Looking for Love

by

Cynthia Breeding

The Sixties: Nostalgia Road

The Wild Rose Press, Inc.
PO Box 708
Adams Basin, NY 14410-0708
Visit us at www.thewildrosepress.com

Publishing History
First Edition, 2025
Trade Paperback ISBN 978-1-5092-6225-0
Digital ISBN 978-1-5092-6226-7

The Sixties: Nostalgia Road
Previously Published by Highland Press 2014
Published in the United States of America

**Books by Cynthia Breeding
published by The Wild Rose Press, Inc.**

Historical Novels:

The Templar's Woman
Knight of Rosslyn (sequel to *The Templar's Woman*)
The Last Pirates
Knight of the Red Rose
The Viking's Yuletide Woman
Gunslinger

~

Ghosts of Culloden series:
Highlander Unleashed
Highlander Untamed
Highlander Unconquered

~

Nostalgia Road: The Sixties series:
Looking for Love
Summer of Love
The Love Beat Goes On

~

Contemporary Novels:

Bedroom Blarney
Night Prey
Cruising along Nostalgia Lane
Christmas Dreams (a time travel)

Prologue

It was the best of times...
It was the worst of times...
　　　　　　~Charles Dickens, 1859

Who knew the same could be said a little over a hundred years later? The decade heralded the Civil Rights Movement, Vietnam, the second "British Invasion" and the era of love-and-peace, Hippie style. Some say if you can remember the Sixties, you weren't really there...

****

Summer, Present Day

Every time Jo Thompson looked in a mirror she was reminded the days had long passed when she wouldn't trust anyone over thirty. While her hair was still thick, silver streaks had begun to appear, coinciding with crinkles around her eyes and a distinct sagging of body parts that used to look fantastic in a bikini. Nowadays, she tended to wear a caftan while sitting on her condo's balcony, sipping frozen margaritas.

Perhaps that was the point. *Her* generation still believed in Margaritaville. Baby Boomers weren't going to go into retirement easily, content to play bingo or shuffleboard. After all, it was her generation that discovered drugs, sex, and rock-and-roll. Well, perhaps not *discovered* those things, but certainly, her generation had revolutionized society even if these days the drugs tended to be meds for aches and pains and the sex—depending on luck—sporadic at best.

But the music…the music lived on. The bands of the Sixties were still touring fifty years later. And perhaps, just maybe, in today's generation of Twitter, Instagram, and You Tube, kids could relate to the music. No matter the age…music made a connection.

Jo smiled as she watched the teenagers splashing each other on the Gulf shore beach, their bodies tanned and toned, not paying any attention to the "old folks" who had been part of the Pepsi generation.

In the words of musician David Essex, *Rock On.*

Chapter One

Summer, 1963

Jo Thompson switched off her transistor radio, which had nothing but static this far from a city, and slid it into her white plastic purse. The last song she'd heard with any clarity had been Jan and Dean's *Surf City*. She was a long way from any ocean. Jo looked out the dust-covered window of the bus as it rolled along endless miles of Heartland highway flanked by sprouting fields of corn, and she wiped her brow with a lace-trimmed handkerchief. For early June, the weather was already hot. In any event, her linen shift-dress was wrinkled and her white flats needed polishing, but maybe her Minnesota cousins wouldn't notice.

"It is unusually hot, isn't it?" a middle-aged lady sitting across from her asked. "I hope this doesn't mean we're in for a sweltering summer. We had a really cold winter, don't you know. Ice and snow right into April. It would serve a body well to have something in between, but I guess the good Lord don't see it that way."

Jo blinked. She wasn't used to having perfect strangers talk to her. "I guess not."

The lady smiled. "You're not from around here, are you?"

"No. New York. Brooklyn, actually."

The woman raised both eyebrows. "You're a mite

young to be traveling so far by yourself, aren't you?"

"I'm thirteen."

"Just a baby. What are you doing way out here?"

The woman certainly asked a lot of questions. "My parents are on a dig in Columbia—they're archeologists," she added when the woman looked confused. "I'm staying with my aunt for the summer."

"Where does your aunt live?"

"Middletown."

"Don't know anyone there since it's a stretch down the road from me." The lady gathered up her things as the bus began slowing down. "Well, the next stop's mine. You take care."

"Thank you. I will."

Jo watched as the woman stepped off the bus, thinking how different the Midwest was from New York. No one would even think of starting up that kind of conversation in Brooklyn.

The bus lurched and moved on. Jo turned her attention back to the countryside, dotted with farms with white wood-frame houses and red barns. So much open space. She hoped she'd be able to get radio reception in Middletown. How could she go an entire three months without listening to the Beach Boys, Dion, the Drifters, Frankie Valli, and Neil Sedaka? She loved music…it spoke to her like a second language.

She sighed. What would her cousins, Wendy and Mary Anne Wade, be like now? Wendy was her age and Mary Anne a year older. It had been three years since she'd seen them, and that visit had ended in a spat that had parents pulling them apart with stern warnings that girls did not fight.

They had called her a sissy just because she was

scared of bugs and frogs and snakes. They'd made fun of the movie star magazines she'd brought along and laughed when she said she wanted to be an actress like Doris Day or Connie Francis.

Remembering the taunts, Jo blinked back the sudden sting of tears. Even though her mother always said her thick, red-gold hair was pretty as a bright penny and her father called her his beautiful little princess, she hadn't seen anything spectacular when she looked in the mirror. Her face was ordinary, save for her green eyes, which tilted slightly at the corners. Wendy had said she looked like a cat and then both cousins had taken to "meowing" at her. She had wanted to growl like a dog at them for that, but then she'd thought of how Doris or Connie would handle the situation and she'd just lifted her chin and given them a bright smile—which seemed to annoy her cousins to no end.

Secretly, Jo knew it was silly to want to be an actress. She was far too shy to get on a stage or anything like that, but it was comforting to pretend to be someone else sometimes. When she'd accidentally seen *Butterfield 8*—she'd gone to the wrong movie door—she hadn't quite understood what was going on, but she loved the way Elizabeth Taylor stuck up for herself and the neat clothes she wore. *The Misfits* was Jo's favorite, though, because she liked how brave Marilyn Monroe was, taking a stance about bucking straps on rodeo horses and freeing wild mustangs. Jo loved horses.

As the bus lumbered to a stop in front of a general store with a wood shingle announcing this was Middletown, Minnesota, Jo stood, put on her wrist-length gloves, and attempted to smooth the wrinkles from her dress. If Marilyn and Elizabeth could stand up for themselves, so could she.

All she needed to do was pretend.

The bright sunlight after the dim interior of the bus nearly blinded her and then she was engulfed in her aunt's warm hug. Aunt Vivian smelled of spring flowers and freshly baked bread. Jo remembered then how much time her aunt had spent in the kitchen on the last visit. Her mother said it was because Aunt Viv had lost her husband to cancer a few months before and baking kept her busy.

"Joleen! It's so good to see you again! We are so glad you'll be spending the summer with us." Her aunt stepped away and gestured. "You remember Wendy and Mary Anne, don't you?"

Jo looked tentatively in their direction. Wendy wore blue jeans, tennis shoes and a baggy T-shirt, her brown hair pulled back haphazardly in a ponytail. She squinted her blue eyes slightly as she looked over Jo's travelling clothes. "This isn't Sunday. Why are you dressed like that?"

"Joleen looks very nice," Aunt Viv said before Jo could answer. "Dressing up a bit lets everyone know she's a lady."

Wendy gave an unladylike snort.

Jo's gaze moved to Mary Anne, but she couldn't tell what her cousin was thinking because her eyes were covered with huge sunglasses. Foster Grants, probably. What did catch Jo's attention, however, was a white streak—a curl actually—that Mary Anne had put in her dark hair on the left side. Jo's mother always said girls who bleached their hair had loose morals, although Jo didn't quite understand what that meant. Still, it wasn't polite to stare. In contrast to Wendy, Mary Anne wore a well-fitting sundress that showed off the beginning of a bosom—she wore lipstick, too, and her fingernails were painted red. Jo blinked and forced her attention back to her aunt.

"I hope I won't be any trouble."

"Nonsense!" Aunt Viv picked up one of Jo's two suitcases and headed toward a car parked across the street. "The girls can use some company."

"Is she going to help us with the chores?" Wendy asked.

Aunt Viv frowned at the question. "We'll see."

"I'll be glad to help," Jo said.

"We'll worry about that tomorrow," Aunt Viv replied. "You must be tired from the long ride."

Jo was, but she didn't want to admit it. She didn't want to be called a sissy again. Wendy had already criticized her dress. Mary Anne, other than saying a bored "hello," ignored her. Now, her cousin held back instead of getting in the car.

"I need to stay in town," Mary Anne said. "Bob wanted to show me his new car."

Aunt Viv shook her head. "I don't want you chasing boys. If Bob wants to show you his car, he can drive out to the farm like a gentleman."

Mary Anne pouted. "All my friends live in town."

"And we live only three miles out," Aunt Viv answered. "Now, in the car."

"*Mother*."

"Don't use that tone of voice, young lady," Aunt Viv said. "Get in the car."

Mary Anne's pout became more pronounced as she threw herself into the back seat. Wendy took the front beside her mother and didn't turn around, so Jo was left to look at the countryside in silence—save for the crunching of gravel beneath the tires—for the short ride to the farm. Not that she minded. The fields were mostly black with crops just beginning to show in neatly plowed rows. Copses of leafy green trees dotted the gently rolling hills. As they neared the farm, Jo could see the sun reflecting silver off a small lake near the turn-off to the farm. Perhaps she could go swimming there.

As her aunt drove to the front of the wooden farmhouse, Jo's attention focused across the yard. In the paddock next to the barn, three horses—a bay, a sorrel and a grey—raised their heads to watch the car come to a stop.

Horses. There hadn't been any on her last visit. Summer vacation was already looking better.

Jo could barely contain her excitement on seeing the horses and wanted to rush right over to the fence, but instead she followed her aunt inside the house and up the stairs to the second floor. The farmhouse was a large one, built in the early 1900s when multi-generational families lived together, so she had been given her own bedroom. She looked around as she set down her suitcases. The pale yellow walls made it feel sunshiny, and white organdy curtains swayed from the gentle breeze through the open window. The room wasn't large, but the single bed was covered with a colorful, hand-quilted coverlet. A wooden wardrobe, painted white, served as a closet and a comfortable-looking chair upholstered in gold corduroy sat next to a small table. Overall, the room felt cozy. "It's very pretty. I like the quilt."

"Thank you. I took up quilting several years ago." Aunt Viv smiled. "Now why don't we go downstairs and join the girls? They've probably already devoured half the chocolate chip cookies I baked this morning."

Wendy and Mary Anne sat at the kitchen table with a half-empty plate of cookies between them. A pitcher of lemonade, the glass frosty from the refrigerator, stood next to the plate. Aunt Viv took two glasses from the cupboard and poured drinks for herself and Jo.

"Help yourself to cookies."

"But leave some for Luke." Wendy licked her fingers.

"Who is Luke?" Jo took a small cookie from the plate.

"Luke Roundtree. His parents own the next farm over," Aunt Viv said. "He rides over every day to help me with the heavier chores."

Jo's ears perked up. "Rides?"

"His horse, Silver Chief, is the grey in the paddock," Aunt Viv replied.

"Named for the Lone Ranger's horse."

"I'm surprised he isn't riding a pinto like Tonto," Mary Anne said.

Wendy ignored her sister. "Silver is hard to handle."

"He's beautiful, though." Jo looked at Wendy and Mary Anne. "How about the other two horses? Are they yours?"

"I don't ride," Mary Anne said. "Horses smell."

Jo had only been to public stables in Brooklyn, but she loved the smell of horses—and leather and hay too. She could probably spend hours in the barn.

Wendy rolled her eyes at her sister. "The bay is mine. His name is Jupiter."

"And the mare is mine," Aunt Viv said, "although I don't have much time for riding what with keeping the farm going. Do you ride, Jo?"

"Oh, yes!" Jo's voice almost squeaked in her excitement.

"How well?" Wendy asked.

"I…I've ridden some," Jo replied. Most of it had been at a walk or post, since the horses weren't allowed to run in New York parks, but her cousins didn't need to know.

Aunt Viv turned to Jo. "Flame—my mare—has an easy disposition. She'll be fine for you if you want to exercise her for me."

"Oh, yes!" Jo exclaimed again. "I would love to!"

"Just don't get any ideas about Silver," Wendy said as the outside door to the kitchen opened.

A boy with the blackest hair Jo had ever seen came into the kitchen. Although cut short, it nearly glistened blue. He wasn't much taller than she was, but the T-shirt clinging to him revealed developing muscles. An athlete, she guessed, maybe a couple of years older than herself.

He stopped halfway to the table, noticing her for the first time. Dark brows rose over startling clear hazel eyes. "I didn't know you had a visitor."

"My niece from New York, Jo Thompson," Aunt Viv filled in. "She will be spending the summer with us."

Luke helped himself to a cookie and smiled, revealing a dimple in one cheek. "Welcome to Minnesota."

"Thank you." Jo felt like a dolt since she couldn't think of another thing to say.

"She loves to ride," Aunt Viv added.

Luke's grin widened. "Then we'll be friends."

Jo swallowed and nodded. Her mouth—or brain—didn't seem to be working, for some reason.

"Don't get any ideas about riding Jupiter or Silver

though," Wendy said, bringing Jo back to her senses.

"N...no, of course not. I'll be happy with Flame," Jo stammered.

Luke gave Wendy a quizzical look, then took another cookie and headed back to the door. "Better go. I still have work to do." He nodded toward Jo. "I'll look forward to riding with you."

"Um...yes. Me too." Jo managed to say, but Luke was already out the door.

She took a sip of her lemonade, wondering why Wendy was watching her so intently. Even Mary Anne was giving her a funny look and she wondered if she had cookie crumbs on her chin. She swiped at it, mortified that maybe Luke had seen, but her hand came away clean. She frowned slightly. Maybe her cousins were just weird.

Yeah, that must be it. They were weird.

Chapter Two

Jo didn't think she'd be able to sleep last night, since Aunt Viv had promised she could go riding in the morning, but by the time she'd gone to bed she'd fallen into a dreamless sleep. If anyone had tried to waken her, she'd have responded like those odd-eyed kids in *Children Of The Damned* walking through cornfields, unaware of anything.

But she felt great this morning! Even better, her transistor radio picked up a signal from a Minneapolis station. Jo hummed along to *Blowin' In The Wind* as she got dressed. Actually, the wind *was* blowing in, since she'd left the window open last night. The air smelled fresher here, kind of like Prospect Park in Brooklyn did after a heavy spring rain, only earthier. A slight scent of barn—hay and animals—wafted across the yard, reminding Jo the horses were waiting.

She made quick work of brushing her teeth and washing her face in the bathroom at the end of the hall. Pulling her long hair back into a ponytail, Jo wished she had some lipstick, but her mother had said she was too young, even for the kind that looked clear but turned light pink once it was on. After her stupid inability to talk to Luke yesterday, she didn't want him to think she was a complete square. Maybe—if she could get Mary Anne to be friends—she could borrow some cosmetics before the summer was over. Putting the thought aside, Jo rushed downstairs.

Aunt Viv turned from the stove where she was flipping pancakes and smiled. "You're just in time, dear. Go ahead and have a seat."

"We don't usually have pancakes," Wendy said as she drained a glass of orange juice. "It's too much trouble."

"Well, today is special." Aunt Viv brought a hot, tall stack to the table and sat down. "It's Jo's first day with us."

"Is she going to help us clean up the kitchen?" Wendy poured syrup over several cakes.

Aunt Viv frowned. "Mind your manners, Wendy."

"I'll be glad to help," Jo said, although wistfully thinking it would delay getting to the horses.

"I'll work out a schedule of chores later," her aunt replied. "For today, you just relax and explore the farm." She plunked down a generous three cakes for Jo and then passed the plate to Mary Anne who shook her head. "You aren't eating?"

"I have to watch my calories," Mary Anne answered and took a sip of coffee and then tried to hide her grimace.

Jo didn't know how Mary Anne could drink that stuff. Even when it was loaded with milk and sugar, it still tasted awful. Her mother had told her it was an acquired taste, but Jo doubted she'd ever like it. She reached for her juice instead and then turned her attention to topping off the pancakes.

With the first bite, Jo moaned with pure pleasure. The melted butter had a sweetness that blended with the maple syrup, while the cakes were light and fluffy and practically melted in her mouth.

"Is something wrong?" Aunt Viv had a look of concern on her face.

"No! Not at all," Jo answered when she had swallowed. "These are delicious! I've never had anything like these."

"Ah, well." The furrow left Aunt Viv's forehead. "It's the farm-fresh eggs that do it. The butter is churned at the local creamery in town."

Jo had never given much thought to where butter came from, other than knowing it appeared in grocery stores in wax-wrapped rectangles, four-to-a-box.

"We get our ice cream from there, too." Wendy's tone was almost challenging.

"Is this a place I can visit?" Jo asked, taking another mouthful and savoring it.

"Of course," Aunt Viv said. "Mr. Larsen, the owner, loves to talk to visitors. He'll even give you a free sample and show you around, if you like."

"I'd like that a lot!"

Mary Anne took another sip of her coffee. "Ice cream is fattening."

Wendy stuck her tongue out at her sister. "Good. I'll eat yours then."

"*Whatever.*"

"Girls!"

They both glanced at their mother, and then Mary Anne looked at the ceiling while Wendy helped herself to another pancake. Jo wondered if her cousins argued a lot. She put a smile on her face, like Doris Day would. "Let me help you clean up, Aunt Viv."

"Not necessary." Her aunt pushed her chair back and stood. "Wendy and Mary Anne will do it since they've decided they must quibble at the table." She held a hand out to Jo. "You and I will go to the stables and saddle the horses."

Jo didn't miss the dark looks she got from her cousins as she followed their mother out the door. She had a feeling she'd just made a mistake, but she didn't know how to correct it.

Jo forgot the concern when she entered the stable moments later. The interior was cool and smelled slightly musty of straw. Dust motes floated on the rays of filtered sunlight coming in from the big double doors open at each end. The warm smell of horses and leather mingled in the air as well. Soft nickers greeted Aunt Viv as Jupiter and Flame stuck their heads over the half-doors of their stalls.

"I think for today, I'll just have you ride in the paddock." Aunt Viv opened the stall and took hold of Flame's halter. "I'd like to see how well you ride before we start down the road and through the fields." She led the mare out and hooked her to the tether on the wall. Then she reached into a pocket of her shirt and brought out a slice of apple. "Here. Go ahead and make friends."

Jo took the apple slice. The mare's ears flicked forward as she turned her head, her dark, liquid eyes watching with interest.

"You're beautiful," Jo said softly, running her hand along the glossy neck. She put the piece of apple in her palm and held out her hand. The mare delicately accepted the morsel, her soft muzzle tickling Jo's skin, and Jo grinned. "I think she likes me."

"Here." Aunt Viv handed Jo a horse brush. "She'll like you even more if you use this. Just do her neck and back for now. We'll curry her later."

Jo took it eagerly. She had always wanted to do this

in New York—take care of the animal—but the horses were rented by the hour and stayed saddled. Finally, she was having a chance to really get to know the horse. The mare blew contentedly through her nose and let her head droop in relaxation. Jo would have been happy to continue for hours. Finally, at last! She was taking care of a horse!

Aunt Viv handed her another slice of apple for Flame. "Do you know how to saddle a horse?"

"I think so," she answered after the mare had devoured the treat. Jo had never done it, but she had watched closely at the public stables in New York. It hadn't seemed too difficult.

"Okay." Aunt Viv led her over to an empty stall where two saddles perched on sawhorses. "That one is Flame's."

Jo blinked. The saddle was huge, with a horn in front and big stirrups. She should have realized it would be a Western saddle, out here in Minnesota. As she pulled it off the rack, her knees almost buckled. It was much heavier that the small, flat English saddles on the horses in the city. Jo tripped on the leather strap attached to the girth and stumbled against the wall. She heard a snicker and realized Wendy had come to the barn to watch. Bravely, Jo managed to slog her way toward Flame, trying to sidestep the dangling strap.

"Just lay the saddle down for a minute." Aunt Viv followed Jo with the saddle blanket. "This goes on first." She demonstrated how far forward to place the blanket and then turned to the saddle, flipping the girth and strap over the saddle and then folding the stirrup skirt over the seat as well. "If you do this first, it will be easier to pull the saddle off the rack as well as place it on the horse's back." Aunt Viv held it out to Jo. "Go ahead."

Suddenly the horse looked a lot taller and Jo hoped she could lift the saddle high enough to actually get it on Flame's back. She heard another snicker and clenched her teeth. Taking a deep breath, she hoisted the saddle and then exhaled in relief that it was actually in place.

"Good." Aunt Viv came forward, flipping the girth and stirrup over to the other side and showing Jo how to tighten the girth. By the time they finished, Jo realized Wendy had already saddled Jupiter and stood waiting.

"How far do you want me to ride with her?" Wendy asked as they led the horses outside.

"We're going to stay in the paddock today," her mother answered.

Jo looked around for the mounting block. She was about to ask where it was when she saw Wendy gather the reins, put a foot in Jupiter's stirrup, and swing herself up. Jo bit her lip. Of course, that was the western way of mounting. What was wrong with her anyway? She watched *Bonanza* and *Rawhide*—she never could decide if Little Joe or Rowdy Yates was cuter—and other TV westerns on a regular basis. Cowboys didn't use mounting blocks. If she was going to ride Western, she needed to get the hang of it. Jo lifted her foot to place it in the stirrup, but Flame edged away.

"Tighten the right rein. It'll keep Flame's head straight and she won't dance," Aunt Viv said from behind her.

Thankful that her aunt couldn't see the blush Jo knew was covering her face, she tried it. To her surprise, Flame stood perfectly still as Jo pushed off the ground with her right foot. She landed in the saddle—not very gracefully—but at least astride.

They moved around to the side of the barn and Aunt Viv opened the gate to the paddock. Wendy surged through, kicking Jupiter to a canter toward the jumps at the far end. Jo watched in fascination as the big gelding took the first low jump easily and then gathered himself to do two in a row and lastly a triple bar. Wendy turned and cantered back, not slowing until she was close enough for Flame to toss her head and prance sideways.

Her aunt frowned at Wendy. Jo knew her cousin was showing off, but she had to admire what she had just seen. "Do you think I can learn to jump?"

"We'll see," Aunt Viv said pragmatically. "Why don't you walk, trot, and canter in a circle for now?"

Jo pressed her heels to Flame's flanks and pulled on the right rein. The mare tossed her head and didn't move. "What's wrong?"

Her aunt moved toward her as Wendy giggled. She gave her daughter a look that made her quit. "Flame's used to neck-reining," she said to Jo. "If you want her to go right, you press the left rein against her neck."

"Oh." Jo felt her face heat again. How stupid could she be?

"Go ahead," her aunt encouraged her. "Try it."

Using the reins correctly this time, Flame moved willingly in a circle. They walked it twice and then Jo tapped the mare's flank to trot. Flame obeyed, but Jo found herself bouncing. She tried to grip the saddle with her legs, but there were no knee puffs as in the English saddle to assist her with position or allow her to post properly. Instead, she slipped around the seat, jarring her back with each step.

Wendy laughed as Jo halted Flame. "What in the world are you doing?"

Jo knew her face must match the red color of Flame's coat, but she met her cousin's gaze. "I was trying to post."

"Post? What in the world is that?"

Suddenly, a male voice answered from the edge of the paddock. "Posting is an English method of riding the trot."

Jo swiveled her head at the sound, then quickly looked away. Luke stood on the other side of the fence, his arms folded along the top. How long had he been there? For sure, he'd seen her bouncing all over the place like she'd never been on a horse before. How embarrassing.

Wendy furrowed her brows. "These aren't English horses."

"No matter." Luke vaulted onto the fence to perch on the rail, the toe of one boot hooked behind a lower plank. "It's a pretty gait to watch. You should learn how to do it."

Wendy's frown deepened. "I don't want to ride English style."

Luke shrugged. "If you want to do anything with jumping, you'll have to learn someday. That's the style used at horse shows. Since Jo seems to know it, maybe she could give you some pointers."

Wendy's chin lifted. Instead of answering, she turned Jupiter toward the jumps. As she cantered away, Jo felt pretty sure she wouldn't be giving her cousin any pointers.

****

Shutting the door to her room, Jo was glad to be alone finally. Although it wasn't all that late, the day had been tiring...and puzzling. After Wendy had ridden off in a huff this morning, Jo hadn't seen her all afternoon and she thought her cousin was mad at her. But then, Wendy had surprised her by being a Chatty-Cathy at dinner—only they called the evening meal "supper" here and "dinner" meant lunch. Mary Anne had pretty much ignored both of them. Jo suspected her older cousin was stuck-up because she would be in high school next year. Maybe, though, Wendy would become her friend.

About to get undressed for the night and crawl into bed, Jo heard a light knock on her door. Actually, it sounded more like someone scratching. Curious, she opened it to find Wendy in the hallway.

"I want to show you something."

"Sure. What?"

Wendy looked over her shoulder as if checking to see if anyone was there. "You'll have to come with me."

"To where?"

"To a secret place I like to go. It's not far from here."

Jo frowned. "It's almost dark."

"Phooey. It's June. We have another hour before it gets dark."

If her cousin was trying to be friends, Jo didn't want to spoil that. Tired as she was, she smiled and nodded. "Okay."

"Great! We'll have to be quiet though, because I don't want Mary Anne following us."

Jo didn't think Mary Anne would be interested in anything they did, but she didn't say it. If Wendy wanted to share her "secret place" with Jo, she should be happy.

"Should we tell your mom we're leaving?"

Wendy shook her head. "Mom already went to bed. She had one of her headaches so I don't want to bother her."

Aunt Viv always seemed so cheerful. But then, Jo had only been here a couple of days. It couldn't be easy, running a farm by herself. "Okay."

Once outside, Wendy stayed close to the side of the house, then cut across the yard behind the hedge that bordered the farm house and past the barn.

"How far is this place?"

"About two miles if we follow the road," Wendy answered, "but it's quicker if we cut through the trees."

Jo looked at the tree line not far away. Most farms had groves on the north side to protect the buildings from blowing snow and harsh winter winds, but since her aunt's farm was close to the small lake fed by a river, the mass of trees was more like a forest behind the house.

"Can we get lost in there?"

"There's a trail." Wendy looked at her. "You aren't scared, are you?"

"No. Of course not."

"It's not like we have bears or bobcats like they do Up North," Wendy said as they walked into the woods. "We can hear wolves sometimes, but I've never seen one."

"Wolves?"

"Yeah, but don't worry. They hunt in the daytime and, like I said, I've never seen one. Don't be such a scaredy cat."

"I...I'm not." Jo followed Wendy through what seemed like a maze of twists and turns. She could see a trail of sorts, but inside the forest, it was definitely getting dark. She wanted to ask how much farther, but bit her lip. Wendy probably already thought she was a sissy.

A short time later, Wendy stopped abruptly at what

looked like another path joining the one they were on. "You don't want to go down there." She pointed to the other trail. "It leads to the old bridge that used to cross the river."

"So? Why would I want to go there?"

Wendy shrugged. "It's kind of a popular hangout for high school couples. I'm just telling you in case you hear stories."

"Stories?"

"Yeah. About twenty years ago, old Mr. Larsen's son ran away with a girl. They were going to get married, only the bridge had rotten boards and their car crashed into the river and the girl drowned."

"How horrible! Did the boy survive?"

"Yeah. He joined the Army and moved away," Wendy said as she started walking again. "Some say you can hear the girl crying at night under the bridge."

"Don't be silly."

"I'm not," Wendy answered. "They say on the anniversary of the crash, the girl walks the old bridge, looking for couples making out, and tries to pull the girl into the water with her."

"I don't believe it—it's just some made-up story."

"Maybe." Wendy shrugged again. "There have been several drownings over the years though."

Jo was pretty sure Wendy was just trying to scare her. Still, she felt relieved when they came to a small clearing where twilight still filled the air. "Is this the place?"

"Sort of." Wendy pointed to a stand of evergreens whose lowest branches nearly touched the ground. "It's over there."

Once they crossed the small glade and rounded the

trees, Jo gasped as she saw a small stone hut with a door hanging off one hinge and a lean-to big enough for a horse. "How did you find this? It's totally hidden from view!"

"I know. It's neat, isn't it?"

"Yes!" Jo eyed the broken door. "Does someone live in it?"

"Nope. Or at least, not for a long time. It was probably a fishing hut once, since it's close to the river."

"But how did you find it?" Jo asked again.

Wendy gave her a sly look. "Actually, Luke found it when he was hiking. He showed it to me. We come here sometimes."

Jo was suddenly glad it was getting dark so Wendy wouldn't see her blush. Was that why her cousin had brought her here? Was Luke her boyfriend? Jo hadn't thought of that. Luke had been friendly this morning, but he hadn't flirted.

"Are...are you dating Luke?"

Wendy hesitated and then smiled. "Mom says I'm too young to actually date..." She let her voice trail off and then changed the subject. "Let's go inside."

Jo followed her through the open door. A large hearth took up most of the space along one wall. Filled oil lamps hung on either side. Nearby, several neatly folded quilts were laid on a cot. Across the room was a wooden table with two chairs. A cupboard held an assortment of dishes and cups and candles, and several large tins stood on the counter. Jo assumed there was probably food inside.

"Does Luke...do you use this often?"

Wendy gave her that secretive smile again. "Luke started high school last year and was busy with sports, but we use it when we can."

We. Wendy had said "we." Maybe they weren't dating, but that meant they were a...a *thing*. Jo felt so stupid for thinking maybe Luke would be interested in her.

"Sit down," Wendy said. "I'm going to go look for some firewood."

"We're going to stay long enough to build a fire?"

"No, we have to get back. I just want to bring some in so it will be dry for...for the next time we come here."

We. Did Wendy mean herself and Jo? Or Luke? "Okay."

Jo sat at the table, trying not to think about what "we" meant. She wasn't old enough to date either, but that didn't mean she didn't notice boys. And Luke was cute...as cute as Ricky Nelson even. She thought of his song *Poor Little Fool*. Maybe that described her instead.

She pushed the thought out of her mind and wondered what was keeping Wendy. They really needed to be getting back.

And then she heard the wolf howl.

Chapter Three

Jo froze. A wolf howling? It was probably a dog. That had to be it. She was letting her imagination run away with her after what Wendy had said about wolves and haunted bridges and all.

Still, it wouldn't hurt to close the door. She forced herself to move and then the howl came again. Closer this time. Jo crossed the small room in four strides. As she grabbed the door handle to push it shut, the remaining rusty hinge broke and the door fell flat. Jo stared at it, as though it might right itself. Her mind registered there was no barrier between her and the wolf now. She looked quickly around the area outside, but the evergreens blocked her vision from whatever could be out there. Did she hear something rustling on the other side of the trees?

And where was Wendy? How far had she gone to get firewood? Had she been attacked by the animal? Was that why she wasn't back? Jo wasn't sure how much time had passed, but it was definitely dark now. Would they even be able to find their way home? The trail was barely visible in light. She knew she'd get hopelessly lost if she even attempted it. Besides, she couldn't leave Wendy.

But where was Wendy?

Jo struggled with the heavy door, trying to prop it sideways against the opening and then realized a wolf—or wild dog—could easily jump over it. The lean-to outside wouldn't offer any more protection since it was completely open on one side, meant to shelter a couple of horses tethered to a rail temporarily.

Jo moved back into the hut and surveyed her options. There weren't many. The hearth was big enough to sit in. Maybe if she dragged the table over and put it on its side, it could act as a shield. Better than sitting in a chair waiting to be mauled.

The table was heavier than she thought, but Jo managed to tug and pull on it until she had it next to the big fireplace. She tried to be careful with turning it over, but the weight got to be too much and the table fell on its side with a huge bang. Jo froze again, holding her breath. The noise was loud enough to attract anything that hunted prey. She listened for a snarl, or something running through the bushes, but all was silent.

Wedging herself behind the table, Jo managed to squat down into the space the hearth provided and maneuvered the table a tad closer. She looked at her barrier, rather proud of herself. Only a few inches of space remained between the side edge of the table and the top of the hearth. She was safe for now—and then she heard rustling outside. Jo didn't dare move, but her blood pounded so loudly in her ears, she could hardly hear anything else. She strained to listen. Yes, something was coming closer.

Jo heard a crash outside and the broken door being moved. Then silence. Slowly, Jo peeked out from her hiding place to find Wendy staring at her.

"What in the world are you doing in there?"

She was so relieved to see her cousin she almost cried. "Where have you been?" Jo asked as she crawled out of the hearth.

"Getting firewood, like I said." Wendy pointed to the heap by the fallen door. "Why did you pull it off its hinge?"

"I didn't. At least, I didn't mean to." Jo tried to swipe soot off her white shorts, which only made it worse. Her knees and legs had black streaks, too, from where she had knelt. "I was trying to keep the wolf away."

Wendy looked at her as though she'd lost her mind. "What wolf?"

"The wolf. Didn't you hear it howl?"

"I didn't hear anything."

"But…you must have. It howled twice and sounded close."

"Whatever you say." Wendy sounded totally unconvinced. "We had better get back."

"Now? It's dark. Anything could be out there—"

"Don't be such a sissy," Wendy said. "Nothing is going to attack us."

"But we could get lost."

"I know the way. Besides," she added, "if Mom found out we were gone all night, I'd be in really big trouble. You don't want to get me into trouble, do you?"

"No, but—"

"Come on then," Wendy said and turned around. Not waiting for an answer, she started to run. "We can be home in no time."

"Wait!" Jo called, but her cousin kept going. Jo took a deep breath and followed, hoping the wolf wouldn't give chase.

****

"Where did you get those scratches on your hands?" Aunt Viv asked Jo the next morning at breakfast.

27

Wendy shot her a look that clearly said not to mention last night's venture. Following the narrow trail in the dark at a jog had Jo bumping into tree trunks and swatting at low branches. She wished her aunt hadn't noticed the scratches.

Jo bit her lip. She hated not telling the truth, but she didn't want to get her cousin into trouble when they just might be becoming friends. "I…uh…I went outside last night and noticed the roses on the trellis by my window. It was almost dark and I guess I got too close." Not a total lie. Jo had noticed the flowers earlier when she'd looked out her window.

"The roses have thorns," Wendy said. "They're pretty, but dangerous."

"Dangerous?" Mary Anne laughed and sipped her coffee. "I hardly think a flower is dangerous, Wendy."

"Oh, shut up."

"You shut up."

Aunt Viv sighed. "Girls."

"She started it."

"Did not."

"Enough!"

Mary Anne rolled her eyes and took another sip of coffee while Wendy sulkily attacked her cereal. Aunt Viv turned to Jo. "Would you like to explore the farm today?"

"Oh, yes! That would be wonderful."

"Luke is due any moment. You can take the horses and he'll show you around."

"I'll go too." Wendy pushed her bowl away.

"Good." Her mother smiled at her. "I'm glad you and Jo are getting to be friends."

Jo doubted whether being friends was why Wendy

wanted to go along, but she didn't say anything. Instead, she picked up her utensils and carried them to the sink. "I'll wash the dishes first."

"Thank you, dear, but Wendy and Mary Anne can do them."

"I don't mind."

"I will work out a schedule then," Aunt Viv said, "but today, Wendy and Mary Anne can do them."

"But if Jo wants…" Wendy let the sentence trail off as her mother gave her a stern look. "Oh, okay." She turned to Jo. "Just don't leave without me."

"I won't."

"Come on, Mary Anne. Get with it," Wendy said.

Her sister glanced at her and broke off a piece of toast. "You wash. I'll dry."

"Fine." Wendy stomped over to the sink and turned on the water, grabbing at the dishes already on the counter.

"Don't break them," Aunt Viv said.

Jo decided this might be a good time to go upstairs and change into jeans.

****

Luke rode into the yard just as Jo started to go back downstairs. She paused by the window to watch Silver Chief toss his head and lift his forelegs off the ground as Luke halted him by the hitching post near the barn. The horse was beautiful and had a lot of spirit. Jo wondered if she'd ever be able to handle a horse like that. Luke made it look so easy.

Luke. He really was the cutest boy she'd ever seen. She liked the way his high cheekbones and straight nose gave his face interesting angles. He had a nice smile too, especially when the dimple showed. It gave him a mischievous look. She watched as he dismounted in one easy movement, his T-shirt pulling tight across his shoulders as he flipped the reins over Silver Chief's neck. Wendy said he played sports in high school.

High school. She would just be going into the eighth grade in the fall. High school boys didn't pay attention to girls her age. But then, Wendy was her age too, and her cousin had hinted that Luke and she were a…thing. Were they?

With a start, Jo realized she had been standing there daydreaming. She hurried out her door and down the stairs.

"There she is!" Aunt Viv said as Jo came into the kitchen.

Luke brushed pastry crumbs off his hands and smiled. "Hi."

"What took you so long?" Wendy asked as she looked over Jo's pressed jeans and crisp white Oxford shirt. "Were you ironing that?"

"No," Jo replied uncertainly. "I just folded everything carefully when I packed."

Wendy smirked. "White is going to get dirty."

"It wouldn't hurt you to have a little fashion sense," Mary Anne said to Wendy, who promptly stuck her tongue out at her sister. Ignoring her, Mary Anne went into the living room and turned on the hi-fi. Strains of Eydie Gorme's *Blame It On The Bossa Nova* drifted after them as they made their way out the door.

"Honestly, all Mary Anne thinks about is dancing and make-up," Wendy grumbled as they entered the barn, "and those snooty friends of hers who all think they're big shots because they'll be going to high school next year."

"High school may take them down a notch or two," Luke said, going into Flame's stall and leading out the mare. "Seniors love picking on freshmen."

"Did they pick on you last year?" Jo asked.

Luke shrugged. "I suppose—"

"They didn't dare, after Luke showed them he could defend himself," Wendy interrupted, smiling at Luke as she hitched Jupiter's lead to a ring. "Everyone in town was talking when you gave Hans Olson and Frederick Burke black eyes!"

Luke grimaced. "They are bullies."

"*Sophomore* bullies," Wendy added, "and big."

"Overweight."

"Whatever. It doesn't matter. You showed them!"

"Fighting isn't always the answer," Luke replied. "My dad got really mad at me for that. Grounded me for a week."

"My dad doesn't like fighting either," Jo said, remembering her last visit to Minnesota. Hopefully Wendy and she were grown-up enough now not to repeat that.

"Sounds like you have a smart dad," Luke answered, getting Flame's saddle and putting the blanket over the mare's back.

Wendy gave Jo an annoyed look. "You should saddle your own horse."

Jo felt her cheeks warm. What had she been thinking, standing there like some princess wanting to be waited on? "You're right! Here, let me do it."

"The saddle's pretty heavy," Luke said.

Jo remembered. She hoped she wouldn't make a fool of herself trying to lift it, but Wendy was right. She should be able to saddle her own horse. "Aunt Viv showed me how to handle it."

"All right." Luke pulled the girth strap and stirrup leather over the seat and held the saddle out.

Jo took hold of the pommel with her left hand and the cantle with her right. As she did, her fingers brushed against Luke's. She nearly dropped the saddle, not prepared for the tingle that slid all the way up her arms from the touch. Maybe it was the dry air inside the barn. Jo sometimes got a shock when she walked across carpet at home and then took hold of a doorknob.

Luke's eyes widened slightly. Had he noticed something too? Jo suddenly realized they were both still holding onto the saddle. Heat flared in her face.

As though Luke realized the same thing, he moved suddenly. "Here. Let me."

With ease, he swung the saddle over Flame, then turned to reach under the horse's belly for the girth and secured it to the metal loop.

An odd sound came from Wendy, but when Jo looked at her, she had her back to them, busying herself with Jupiter's saddle.

Luke didn't seem to notice. "Did Mrs. Wade show you how to check for proper tightness of the girth?"

"Ah…no."

"Move over here then." Luke indicated a spot near him. "See if you can slip two fingers beneath the strap."

As Jo stepped closer, she thought she saw Wendy's shoulders stiffen, but she wasn't sure. Luke had swung the left stirrup leather up, so Jo could see how the girth was fastened. Tentatively, she tried to wedge two fingers behind the leather. "It's tight."

"Good. That means the horse didn't hold its breath while I was fastening it."

Jo frowned. "Why would Flame do that?"

"Room." Luke grinned, the dimple showing. "She probably doesn't like a tight belt any more than humans do."

"That makes sense."

"Yeah, but if it's too loose, the saddle will slip. Not good. But you don't want it too tight either, where it pinches the horse." Luke smoothed his hand over Flame's hide. "See how smooth this is? Just right."

Another strange sound came from Wendy, but this time when Jo glanced over, Wendy was looking at Luke. "Are we going to ride or not?"

He hesitated a moment and then nodded. "Yeah. We're going to ride."

Once down the yard road, they turned right onto a gravel road that didn't have much traffic, allowing them to ride abreast most of the time. Jo rode on the edge next to the ditch, with Luke in the middle and Wendy on the other side. He pulled ahead and she fell behind into single file when they did meet a car. Flame didn't seem to notice although Silver pranced and snorted his disapproval of the modern, noisy inconvenience, but Luke kept him steady. Jupiter tossed his head too, but Wendy didn't seem to have a problem handling him. Jo wondered if she'd ever ride as well as either of them.

And Wendy was right about one thing. White did get dirty. Jo's shirt was covered in a fine layer of dust from the few cars that passed. Jo saw Wendy taking note of it, but to her cousin's credit, she said nothing. Jo decided to ignore the dirt too and enjoy the countryside.

Across the road from them were tilled black fields with neatly planted rows of corn and wheat and something Jo didn't recognize but Luke said was soybeans.

"How does your mother handle all this?" Jo asked Wendy.

"Since Dad died, she rents out the acreage."

Jo bit her lip, thinking maybe she shouldn't have asked, but her uncle had been gone two years and Wendy seemed to be okay.

"Mrs. Wade's brother-in-law lives a couple of miles over, but he's military and gone a lot, so it's practical," Luke said. "My dad rents some of the land, as do the Olsens and Burkes since all our property surrounds Mrs. Wade's. Her brother-in-law has a farm about a mile down the road, but his acreage is rented too, since he's in the Army. He may be sent somewhere called Vietnam, I think. Anyway, both ladies have an income this way and don't have to worry about planting crops."

Wendy giggled. "Can you see Mary Anne driving a tractor?"

"Considering the crooked line you steered learning to ride your bike, I can't see you driving one either," Luke teased.

"I was only eight when I learned to ride a bike!" Wendy retorted, but she smiled. "Besides, I beat you racing often enough."

"Only because I let you win."

"You did not!"

Luke grinned. "How do you know?"

Jo watched the interchange. Luke had known Wendy a long time, since they were children. Did he think of her as a girlfriend?

Luke pointed to the other side of the road and Jo realized he was talking to her. "Mrs. Wade's property ends over there." He indicated the stand of trees Jo and

Wendy had gone through on their way to the hidden cabin. "We'll ride around it to the river and then come back along the lakeside."

"Are we going to cross the haunted bridge?" Jo asked.

Luke smiled and glanced at Wendy before answering. "I see you've been filled in on our local legends."

"Wendy told me when she showed me your...the cabin," Jo said.

"Ah, the cabin. I haven't been there in a while, but it's a nice little spot, isn't it?"

"Except for the wolves."

One of his dark brows rose. "Wolves?"

"Well, a wolf. I was inside the cabin when I heard it last night. Wendy was getting firewood," Jo replied, feeling kind of stupid about the whole thing in broad daylight.

Luke gave Wendy an appraising look. "Did you hear anything while you were getting wood?"

"No. Nothing," Wendy said, although her face turned pink. "I think Jo has an overly active imagination."

"Um." Luke grew thoughtful. "Odd that you were outside and didn't hear something that Jo heard inside."

"I didn't hear anything," Wendy said, but her face reddened again. "Nothing."

"It might have been a dog," Jo offered since Wendy seemed uncomfortable with the subject. Maybe her cousin felt guilty over leaving her alone.

"Maybe," Luke answered. "I can't remember the last time a wolf was spotted anywhere near here, but the river does attract wildlife like badgers and bobcats.

Probably better to stay out of the woods at night."

"I will," Jo replied.

Wendy gave her a look that said "sissy" although she didn't voice it.

Jo wasn't a sissy. She wasn't. "I'd like to see the haunted bridge though."

"It's just an old wooden bridge, and it isn't really safe to cross, even on foot." Luke smiled. "But we can go there another day if you really want to."

"I would." Jo felt a fluttering sensation in her stomach. Had Luke just...kind of—sort of—asked her on a date? How exciting! Just the two of them, riding...

And then Luke spoiled her illusion by adding, "And Wendy can show us where she was when you heard the wolf."

Chapter Four

"Turn down the radio, Wendy," Aunt Viv said as she set a stack of grilled cheese sandwiches on the table for the noonday meal, along with potato salad. "We don't need to be listening to bad news while we eat."

"I don't really understand what's happening in Alabama." Wendy lowered the volume on her transistor and laid it on the table. "Why does the governor not want to let two black students into the university?"

"Wasn't Alabama the state where kids and bystanders were sprayed with fire hoses this spring because they were protesting blacks not being able to sit in white areas of restaurants?" Jo asked.

"That's right," Aunt Viv answered. "It's a terrible shame people treat each other that way."

"Maybe it's just Alabama," Wendy commented. "It seems they're always in the news with stuff like that."

"It's not just Alabama," Aunt Viv said. "Maryland, Mississippi, the Carolinas…it's just horrible how Americans can turn on one another."

"Well, I'll bet President Kennedy can fix it," Wendy replied.

"Let's hope so," her mother answered. "Let's hope so."

"Jackie can help him," Jo added. "She's smart and everyone likes her. I love the way she dresses too."

Wendy nodded, turning the volume back up to

Aretha Franklin's *R-E-S-P-E-C-T*.

Aunt Viv smiled at them, but her eyes were sad and Jo wondered why.

****

"Guess what!" Mary Anne burst into the kitchen two days later while Jo and Wendy were finishing breakfast. She waved a letter. "This just came in the mail."

"Great. It's a letter. Could you tell us who it's from?" Wendy chewed her last bite of toast.

"Don't talk with your mouth full." Mary Anne made a face at Wendy. "It's from Tim and Tommy."

"They're our cousins," Wendy explained when Jo gave her an inquiring look. "Their dad's in the Army."

"The man Luke told us about the other day when we were riding?" Jo asked.

"Yeah."

Jo creased her brow. "Why do they write you letters if they live only two miles down the road?"

Wendy giggled. "They don't live down the road."

Furrowing her brow more, Jo felt confused. She didn't know the family. Aunt Viv was her mother's sister, and Uncle Robert had already passed away when Jo visited last time. "They don't? But I thought Luke said—"

"Their mother lives down the road," Mary Anne explained. "Tim and Tommy are twins and my age. They were both in the Foreign Exchange program last year and went to school in England."

"Going to school in England? Wow!" Jo said. "They must really be smart."

"I guess." Mary Anne shrugged. "Their dad, our Uncle Martin, is like a colonel or something in the Army. He arranged it."

"Are you going to tell us what the letter says?" Wendy asked and then made an elaborate gesture of dabbing her mouth with her napkin when Mary Anne glared at her. "I'm through eating."

Mary Anne ignored her and pulled out the single piece of paper. Then she let out a shriek and put a hand to her heart.

"Ouch!" Wendy covered her ears. "Save the theater stuff, will you? What does the letter say?"

"They're on their way home! They'll be here by July Fourth… Oh, my gosh! That's like two weeks away! I have so much to do!" She rushed from the room, taking the letter with her while Wendy shook her head.

"What does she have to do?" Jo asked.

Wendy rolled her eyes. "Who knows? It might take her that long to do her hair and put on her make-up."

Jo raised both eyebrows. "What? You're kidding."

"Well, yeah. But really, it takes her almost that long," Wendy replied, "especially when she's getting ready for a boyfriend."

"Boyfriend?"

"Before they left for England, Tim called Mary Anne his girlfriend."

Jo felt her forehead crease again. "But…aren't they cousins?"

"Sort of. Actually, the twins are adopted."

"Oh." Jo's frown stayed in place. "I don't understand, though. I thought that Bob guy—with the car—was her boyfriend."

"He kinda is—was, I guess, now that Tim is coming back—but Mom doesn't like him. Bob, that is. Not Tim."

"I see," Jo said, although she clearly didn't. It must have showed on her face because Wendy giggled again.

"You will. It's going to get interesting soon."

****

"So how are things going?" Luke asked a few days later as Jo led Flame out of the barn. He'd just arrived and Jo could smell the clean scent of soap from his morning shower. The smell blended with the fresh air and earthiness of tilled fields.

"Pretty well," Jo replied and surprised herself by thinking things really had improved. Mary Anne had stopped her habitual pout about not being allowed to go into town and hang out on a daily basis. Jo supposed that was because her boyfriend—or her *other* boyfriend— was coming home. But the real change had been in Wendy.

She had become much friendlier—or at least not so catty—since Luke had taken both of them to the "haunted" bridge. He had been right…it was nothing more than a rickety wooden bridge with slats gone and most of the railing on one side broken. Nothing seemed scary about it. The river flowed calmly under the old bridge, but Luke said that was deceptive. The water was deep here and the current not visible on the surface. The grassy slope on one side seemed more inviting to couples wanting to make out than to despondent ghosts gliding along the edge of the water, but then, they had gone there on a bright, sunny day. Wendy reminded them the stories had all taken place at night when all sorts of creatures were afoot.

And then, Luke asked Wendy about the wolf.

She'd stuck to her story that she hadn't heard anything, until Luke took them to the cabin and had her retrace her steps. Jo thought he was making too big a deal about the whole thing until he told her if she really had heard a wolf, that meant more were likely, since they were pack animals, and the neighbors needed to know. "Strange that there aren't any tracks though," he'd said.

Wendy had looked at the ground and shuffled her feet. Luke had stood quietly watching her and Jo had watched him, wondering what was going on.

Finally, Wendy confessed she had made the sounds to scare Jo because she thought it would be funny.

Somewhat confused, Jo asked Luke what had gotten him suspicious.

"Just a hunch, plus the fact that this firewood—" Luke pointed to the pile Wendy had dropped at the door "—had been moved only a few feet from where it had been placed the last time I was here."

The realization that not only had Wendy played a trick on her but she'd never been far away from the cabin in the first place made tears well up in Jo's eyes. She'd blinked hard, willing herself not to cry, but some trickled down her cheeks anyway.

"I'm sorry." Wendy threw her arms around Jo and started to cry too.

Luke took one look and went to get the horses.

"Are you going out riding by yourself?" Luke asked now.

Jo shook her head. "Wendy's in the barn saddling Jupiter."

"I wish I could join you guys," Luke said, "but I just came by to see if Mrs. Wade needs anything done before I go help my dad." He turned to walk toward the house and then stopped. "I'm glad you and Wendy are finally friends."

"I'm glad too," Jo said. "Thank you for helping me."

Luke's face turned pink, and for a moment he

hesitated, then he waved his hand. "It wasn't anything," he said and quickly walked away.

****

The twins arrived home two days early, on July 2. Mary Anne screamed as her uncle's Wildcat Buick crunched the gravel on the yard road.

"I'm not ready! I'm not ready! They weren't supposed to be here until the Fourth!" she screeched as she raced up the stairs to her room. "Keep them busy, Wendy!"

Wendy rolled her eyes and shook her head as Jo turned on the hi-fi in the living room to drown out Mary Anne's wailing. "They aren't celebrities, you know!" Wendy called after her sister.

"I can't let them see me like this!"

Jo grinned. "Maybe she thinks she's the celebrity!"

"Probably," Wendy replied as her mother came in from the kitchen, wiping her hands on a dishtowel.

"Whatever is all the racket about?"

"Tommy and Tim are here," Wendy said.

"Oh, my goodness," her mother said as she looked out the window at the car now stopped. "I think we've got some cookies left. I planned on baking pies—"

"It's Tommy and Tim, Mother," Wendy said. "Not rock stars."

"But they've been gone so long," she answered as she hurried to the door, opened it, and then gave them hugs. "Welcome home, boys! Just look at how you've grown!"

For a moment all Jo could see were backs. The twins' father had managed to escape her aunt's hugs, but he was also blocking the view. The boys didn't seem quite as tall as Luke, but they were fourteen, a year younger, if Jo remembered correctly.

Finally, her aunt stepped back and the boys came into the living room. Jo blinked, not sure her eyes weren't playing tricks. The twins were dead-ringers for Troy Donahue with their dark blond hair and green eyes. One of them wore his hair to the side like Troy, but the other had combed his hair forward and down in what looked like…bangs. How strange.

"Hey, Wendy! How's our favorite little cousin?"

"I'm not little anymore!" Wendy retorted and turned to Jo. "This is Tommy," she said and pointed to the twin with bangs. "That's Tim."

"And who might this be?" Tim asked with a slight British accent.

"Oh, sorry. My cousin Jo from New York. She's spending the summer with us."

. Tim smiled at her. "From Manhattan?"

"No. Brooklyn," Jo replied.

"Still the city though," Tim said, looking impressed. "I found London to be quite interesting. We'll have to compare stories."

Tommy snorted. "We were only in London two days, bozo."

Jo noticed Tommy didn't have any trace of an accent although Tim's seemed to be more pronounced as he ignored his brother. "I liked the hustle and bustle."

"Is that the Beach Boys you're listening to?" Tommy interrupted.

"Yeah, *Surfin' USA*," Wendy said. "It's been playing a lot this summer, even if we aren't close to an ocean."

"I missed American music," Tommy said.

"They didn't play it in England?" Jo asked in

surprise.

"Oh, they did, but then this English group, The Beatles, got really popular."

"Beetles?" Wendy giggled. "A group named itself after bugs?"

"No. It's spelled B-E-A-T-les," Tim replied, "as in 'rhythm and beat.' There are four of them and they're cool blokes."

"Yeah, yeah, yeah," Tommy said, "and Tim's been mimicking the accent ever since he heard them."

"I am not!"

"He even wears his hair like them," Tommy snickered.

"It kind of looks like a mop," Wendy said with another giggle.

Tim lifted his chin. "It's very 'in' over there."

"And we're here. In the good old USA," Tommy replied.

"I'm telling you these chaps are going to be big here too. Just wait and see."

"If they can see through all that hair to find their way over here."

"Do they have any albums out?" Jo asked to defuse the situation. Gosh, the twins sounded like Wendy and Mary Anne squabbling.

"One so far," Tim answered.

"What's it called?"

Before he could answer, Mary Anne appeared from the hallway. She'd changed into a sundress with spaghetti straps. Aunt Viv frowned, but Jo wasn't sure if it was because the dress was cut low or whether it was because Mary Anne was wearing red lipstick *and* eyeshadow. She must have helped herself to her mother's perfume as well, because Jo could smell her aunt's *Evening in Paris* all the way across the room.

Tim's eyes lit up appreciatively as she walked toward him slowly, holding his gaze. Jo almost laughed. It looked as though Mary Anne was trying to imitate Ann-Margaret in *Bye-Bye Birdie,* but she just looked funny. Still, Tim didn't seem to mind as she took his hand.

"Let's go out on the porch where we can talk, okay?" Mary Anne asked in a voice that didn't sound like hers either.

"Sure." He followed her to the door and then turned around to look at Jo. "Please, please me."

Jo widened her eyes. "What?"

Tim smiled. "The name of The Beatles' first album. It's *Please, Please Me.*"

Chapter Five

July 4th turned out to be one of those gloriously wonderful days that Aunt Viv said Minnesotans liked to brag about to their neighbors south of the Mason-Dixon who were sweltering in summer heat. The sky was azure blue, dotted with fluffy cotton clouds. A light zephyr breeze from the north kept the temperatures in the 70s. The small lake at the edge of Aunt Viv's property shimmered silvery under the rays of the late afternoon sun, and what looked to Jo like every man, woman, and child in Middletown—along with a various assortment of dogs—had gathered along its grassy edge for a potluck picnic.

Checkered red-and-white vinyl tablecloths covered the trestle tables borrowed from several of the local churches. Some creative soul had draped blue bunting along the fronts of the tables, as well. Jo didn't think she'd ever seen so much food in one place. Salads— German potato with bacon bits, mustard potato, warm sour-cream potato with ham, macaroni and peas, macaroni and cheese, fresh cucumber, ambrosia fruit, Gelatin molds with fruit, and even, hidden toward the back, lettuce and tomato. Two more tables held homemade desserts—from every type of pie and cake imaginable to cookies and peanut-butter bars and lemon squares. A big churn of fresh vanilla ice cream sat beside those treats, along with two rather stern-faced women whose task was keeping the children—and some adults—away from the sweets until later.

But what intrigued Jo the most was something her aunt referred to as "Hot Dish." When Wendy announced her mother was making one and that it had won a blue ribbon at the county fair last year, Jo had asked what it was. Wendy had looked at her blankly and replied, "Hot Dish."

Jo was left to mull over the matter until she arrived at the picnic a short time ago. Apparently, "Hot Dish" was a casserole that included whatever the cooks—depending on their degree of imagination or daring—chose to put in it. The basic ingredients seemed to be egg noodles, ground beef, and tomato sauce, although the delicious aromas wafting in the air above the groaning table told Jo's nose that onions, garlic, and other spices had gone into the recipes, as well. Jo's mouth began to water in anticipation.

"Makes you hungry, doesn't it?" Luke asked from behind her.

Jo jumped, nearly tripping on the uneven ground. Luke's hand caught her arm, steadying her. "Careful there."

Even though he dropped his hand as soon as she'd gotten her balance, Jo felt that strange little tingle shoot up her arm again. She didn't think the air was dry enough for static electricity to cause the sensation. How strange.

Luke gestured, seeming not to notice her reaction. "Your cousin seems to be holding court."

Jo forced her gaze to follow where his finger pointed. Mary Anne sat on a boulder, holding a paper plate with desserts—how had she managed those?—and surrounded by several boys. Tim and Tommy sat to one side of her, and the errant Bob on the other. Jo had only seen Bob sitting in the front seat of his car when he'd come to pick Mary Anne up on a couple of occasions—occasions when her aunt was gone—and now Jo could see why Aunt Viv was skeptical.

Most of the boys wore khaki pants and tucked-in, collared shirts and, with the exception of Tim's mop, sported short crew cuts. Bob looked like something out of a James Dean movie. In fact, he *looked* a little bit like James Dean. Dark hair, slicked back, tight jeans, and a white T-shirt under a black leather jacket, with motorcycle boots. Jo wondered what Mary Anne saw in him.

"You're staring," Luke said.

Jo started. "I was just thinking that Bob doesn't fit in with the rest."

"I guess he doesn't," Luke replied. "He's almost eighteen, older than most of them, and he's not from here."

"Where's he from?"

"Chicago."

"Chicago? Why did his family move out here?"

"They didn't. He got sent here."

"Oh. Kind of like me?"

Luke smiled. "Not exactly. I heard he got into some kind of trouble in the city and he had a choice to come here to live with an uncle or…or face the consequences."

Jo furrowed her brow and then widened her eyes. "You mean jail?"

"I don't know. He didn't say."

"You talk to him?"

Luke shrugged. "He was in my English class last year."

"But...didn't you say he's almost eighteen? Shouldn't he be a senior?"

"Probably. I think he dropped out for a while."

Jo gave Luke a thoughtful look. "It sounds like you know him pretty well."

"Not really. I just remember what it was like when my dad bought the farm when I was in first grade. Bob's uncle moved into town about a year ago. It takes time to make friends...it did me."

"You? I wouldn't think you'd have any trouble. You're so..." Jo stopped, blushing. Holy-moly, she'd almost told him she thought he was really cute. "I mean...little kids usually just get along."

"Some people didn't like the fact that my dad's part Ojibwa."

"Indian?" Jo frowned. "What difference does that make?"

Luke smiled at her. "Back then, some folks felt we should have stayed on the reservation Up North."

"That's ridiculous. Indians were here first. Manhattan Island was named by the Lenni Lenape tribe, for Pete's sake."

He raised an eyebrow. "How do you know that?"

"My parents are archeologists," Jo replied. "They come up with weird stuff. Anyway, everyone around here is so friendly."

Luke looked away. "There are still a few folks who don't feel that way."

"You're kidding." Jo followed his gaze to see it was centered on Tim and Tommy. "You don't mean—"

"Let's just say we've never been friends, okay?" Luke changed the subject abruptly, as Wendy made her way over to them. He pointed to the line that was forming. "We'd better join them before the bowls are empty."

"Sure," Jo said as she and Wendy followed him. It couldn't be true though...what Luke thought. Tim and Tommy seemed so nice.

****

"I didn't get much time to talk to you yesterday at the picnic," Tim said to Jo the next afternoon as they sat in the farmhouse parlor.

Jo looked at him in surprise. Mary Anne was upstairs, finishing getting ready for wherever he and she were going, and Tommy was playing a game of checkers with Wendy on the coffee table. "Why did you want to?"

Tim smiled. "I find you interesting. I want to get to know you better."

Jo pulled her brows together. "Isn't Mary Anne your girlfriend?"

He shrugged. "It appears she has been busy while I have been away. Besides, you are from New York City. I quite like big cities—"

"Would you like some tea to go with the fake accent?" Tommy asked. "We were in London the day we arrived and the day we left. The rest of the time we went to school outside Blackburn, hardly a huge city."

Tim gave his twin an annoyed look. "We were close to Liverpool. *And* we did get to go to that club there, to see the Beatles."

Tommy shook his head and turned back to his checkers game, but Wendy's eyes were wide.

"You went to a club? Like a bar?" she asked. "How did you get in?"

Tim puffed out his chest. "Well, the English are a bit more lenient, and I suppose we looked old enough."

Tommy snickered. "Sean's parents took us. Once."

"Who's Sean?"

"The kid whose house we lived at."

"That must have been interesting," Jo said.

Tim smiled at her again. "Not as interesting as you, though."

Jo felt herself squirm. "I haven't done anything exciting."

"But you live in New York City. That's exciting in itself. Times Square, Broadway, Madison Square Garden, the Empire State Building—"

"Those are all in Manhattan," Jo interrupted, "a good fifteen miles away from where I live."

"Fifteen miles isn't far."

"Not here in the country," Jo replied, "but it would take a good hour or more to get to Manhattan by subway, and my parents would never allow me to go alone."

Tommy looked up curiously. "You've never been to Manhattan, then?"

"Only with my parents. We went to a lot of museums."

"Boring," Tommy replied and moved a checker.

"Did you find the museums boring?" Tim asked.

"I guess not," Jo said. "Mom and Dad are both into that kind of stuff, so they always knew a lot about the background of the things we saw. We went to Central Park, too," she added. "I even got to go riding there once."

"I did a lot of riding while we were in England," Tim replied. "Sean's mom had a Thoroughbred mare that used to be a hunter."

"He fell off twice," Tommy muttered.

Tim frowned. "Only at first. You wouldn't even

try."

"I have a peace treaty with the beasts. I don't ride them and they don't bite me."

Wendy giggled. "Silly. Jupiter would never bite anyone. I'll show you."

"No, thanks."

Ignoring his twin, Tim looked at Jo intently. "Sean's dad said I had excellent hands. He said they were quite sensitive, like I knew what she wanted."

"She?" Jo asked. "Oh…you mean the mare."

"Of course." Tim gave her a slow half-smile. "What did you think I meant?"

Jo was spared the need to give an answer as Mary Anne swept into the room. A cloud of her mother's expensive perfume preceded her, even though she was dressed casually in pedal pushers, an oxford shirt with the tail hanging out, and penny loafers. Jo wondered if Aunt Viv would take to locking up her perfume before the bottle was empty. Then again, her aunt was probably happy Mary Anne was going out with Tim instead of Bob.

"I'm ready," Mary Anne announced. "Shall we go?"

"Sure," Tim said as he stood. His eyes lingered for a moment on Jo. "Later then."

****

Mary Anne was out of sorts a few mornings later at breakfast, slopping coffee over the edge of her mug and practically throwing down her cereal spoon before she pushed away from the table and stomped up the stairs.

"What's wrong with her?" Jo asked.

"She's just mad because Mom told her she couldn't go with Tim and Tommy to Minneapolis today."

"That's a pretty long trip."

Wendy nodded. "Ninety miles, and they're planning to stay overnight at another cousin's house, which is why Mom said no."

So the twins were going to be gone two days. Jo breathed a sigh of relief. They'd come by every afternoon this past week, and Mary Anne always kept Tim waiting in the parlor—something she said girls were supposed to do, although Jo didn't understand why—and while he waited, he watched Jo like a wolf might when stalking his next meal.

Not that Tim actually said or did anything wrong. Wendy and Tommy were in the room too, although usually absorbed in a board game. Still, Tim made Jo uncomfortable and she didn't know why. He seemed to think it funny that she chose to sit on a straight-backed chair next to a potted plant. He'd even given her that half-smile of his and asked if she was hiding back there. Jo still remembered how her face had flamed. She'd made the mistake of sitting on the sofa the second afternoon the twins had come over. Tim had sat much too close to her, although he'd jumped up as soon as Mary Anne could be heard on the stairs.

Wendy hadn't seemed to notice, and Jo decided not to mention it. She'd probably just be thought silly. It wasn't like he'd *touched* her or anything.

But still, it was good the twins would be gone for two days.

****

The morning of the third day, Mary Anne appeared for breakfast all bubbly and cheerful. Jo wasn't sure if it was because Tim would be coming home today or the fact that Mary Anne had snuck out of the house the night before. Jo had heard the revved-up engine of Bob's car on the road after midnight and gone to her window to see Mary Anne running toward his vehicle. Jo hadn't gotten much sleep last night, wondering if she should tell Aunt Viv. Finally, she'd decided to talk to Wendy first.

That worry flew out of her head when Jo heard hooves beating up the yard road. Luke! He hadn't been over since the Fourth because the fields needed cultivating to get rid of weeds. She'd found herself missing him.

"Luke's here!" Wendy exclaimed.

From her cousin's excited tone and the way she pushed her chair back quickly, she must have missed him too. Jo's own elation deflated like a stuck balloon. She and Wendy had become friends since the cabin incident, but that didn't mean anything had changed between Luke and Wendy. "I'll take the dishes into the kitchen and help your mom."

"Thanks!" Wendy said, but she was already half out the door.

By the time Jo got to the stables, Wendy had already saddled Jupiter and was in the paddock. Luke led Flame out. "You didn't have to saddle her."

"No problem. Wendy said she wanted to practice jumping today, and I thought you might like to try."

"I've never done any jumping." Jo looked toward the hurdles set up at the far end of the paddock. "Those look pretty high."

"If you've never jumped, I wouldn't let you start with those," Luke said. "We'll begin with something about a foot high. And first, I'll walk Flame through it a few times to be sure she knows what to do. I wouldn't want you flying over her head if she decides to balk."

Luke lowered the rail on the first jump and spent the

next half hour working with the horse, walking her to it, having her step over, then fastening the reins to the saddle horn and running beside her at a trot, urging her to hop it. Flame soon sensed what he wanted, and in no time gathered her forefeet under her and launched over with a powerful thrust of her haunches. Jo suspected after the ninth or tenth jump that Luke was giving her more time to get over her nerves rather than making sure the horse knew what to do.

"Ready?" he asked.

Jo took a deep breath and moved forward.

"Relax your hands," he said once she was settled in the saddle. "Keep the reins loose so Flame can stretch her neck. Lean forward over the withers, but grip the saddle with your knees." He made her practice the position a few times. "Got it?"

"I…I think so."

"Good. And remember," Luke said as he stepped back. "Trust your horse."

Jo felt Flame's skin shimmy beneath her as the mare's ears twitched back and forth inquiringly. The animal felt her tension and Jo forced herself to relax. The jump wasn't that high, after all, and Flame knew what to do. Walking her horse several paces away, Jo turned, aligned with the jump, and pressed her heels to the mare.

Flame broke into a smooth canter, nodding her head a bit, asking for more rein. Jo loosened the hold and leaned forward. Flame lifted, suspended in air, and then dropped gracefully on the other side, not missing a stride as she cantered off.

Jo had never felt anything so exhilarating in her life. For that airborne moment, it had been like she was riding Pegasus. She turned Flame and trotted back to Luke, laughing. "I want to do it again!"

"Probably not a good idea," Tim said as he stepped from the shadows of the barn.

Jo's laughter faded. She hadn't seen Tim, and apparently neither had Luke because he snapped his head around.

"Why shouldn't Jo jump?" Luke asked.

"It's not that she should not jump," Tim said, disdain in his voice, "but not with that equipment. I would think you would have better sense than to use a Western saddle."

"Mrs. Wade doesn't own any English saddles."

Tim ignored Luke's answer and looked at Jo. "The Western saddle is too heavy and can affect the horse's ability to get the lift it needs." He jerked his thumb toward Luke. "Your *horse master* here should know that."

A muscle twitched in Luke's jaw, and Jo bristled, but before she could retort, Wendy galloped over. "Hey, when did you guys get back?"

"Yesterday," Tim said, "and not a minute too soon, either."

"Mary Anne will be glad to hear that, then," Jo said.

Tim shook his head. "What I meant was, I arrived just in time to save your horses, since someone is obviously encouraging you to jump in Western gear."

"But that's all we've got," Wendy replied.

"Don't worry. I'll have my dad order a pair of English saddles as soon as I get home. He can usually get a discount."

"Oooh! That would be great," Wendy said as she slid off Jupiter.

Jo dismounted as well, noticing Luke had set his

mouth in a tight line. "Maybe we just shouldn't jump. I wouldn't want to hurt the horses."

"Just don't jump until the other saddles get here." Tim smiled at her. "And then I will give you lessons."

"Luke's done a good job," Jo said, and Wendy nodded her agreement, looking somewhat confused.

"Perhaps." Tim shrugged. "But I learned to ride in England, remember. The English know how to jump horses."

"I've changed my mind," Jo said suddenly. "I don't want to learn to jump."

Wendy stared at her. "Why not? It's fun."

"Maybe not that much fun." Jo turned to Luke. "Could you help me brush Flame? She deserves a good grooming."

A corner of Luke's mouth twitched. "Sure." He took the reins and headed for the barn. "Let's go."

"Wait for me!" Wendy said and hurried after them, leaving Tim to glower into empty space.

Chapter Six

Jo hoped that by the time she and Wendy finished grooming the horses, Tim and Mary Anne would have gone to wherever they went to, but she found both of them sitting in the parlor. Mary Anne had a gift-wrapped box on her lap, so Tim must have brought her a present. Jo and Wendy rolled their eyes at each other and moved toward the stairs, but Tim had spotted them in the hallway.

"Jo! Come in and join us," he called.

Jo groaned. "I guess we can't be rude."

"We?" Wendy grinned at her. "I didn't hear him call my name." She quickly hopped up a couple of stairs before Jo could grab her. "You go have fun."

Jo made a face at her cousin's retreating back. Wendy had stuck like glue in the stable when Luke was helping with the horses. Why couldn't she stick around now? Reluctantly, Jo turned toward the parlor. At least, Mary Anne was in there.

"Look what Tim bought me while he was in Minneapolis!" Mary Anne exclaimed as soon as Jo walked in. She held up a bottle of *Fame* cologne. "It's from France!"

From its small size, Jo guessed it was probably expensive, and she wondered how long it would last. At least Aunt Viv would have some *Evening In Paris* left for a while.

"Very nice."

Mary Anne jumped up. "I'm going to the bathroom to wash off what I'm wearing so I can use some of this."

Who knew how long that would take? Jo didn't want to entertain Tim that long. "Why don't you wait until later? I mean, you have a guest—"

"Don't be silly! I'll be right back," she said and dashed off.

"Aren't you going to sit down?" Tim asked after Mary Anne had gone.

"I…uh…yeah, I guess." Jo moved to the straight-backed chair by the potted plant. "That was really nice of you to bring Mary Anne a gift."

"I got tired of smelling her mother's perfume." He put his hand inside his jacket, took out another small package and brought it over to Jo. "I brought you some too."

"I can't accept—"

"Sure you can." Tim unwrapped the bottle and placed it on the small table beside the chair. "All the girls in high school are wearing it."

"Uh…thank you."

"You're welcome." Tim walked back to the sofa and flopped down. "I'll get those saddles ordered as soon as I get home."

"You don't have to—"

"I told you I wouldn't take long!" Mary Anne interrupted as she breezed through the room, a new scent clinging to her. She pounced on the sofa next to Tim and tilted her head sideways, exposing her neck. "Do you like it?"

He bent forward and sniffed appreciatively. "Very much."

"Good!" Mary Anne gave him a big smile. "What were you saying about new saddles?"

"When I got here this morning, Wendy and Jo were both jumping their horses in Western gear." Tim shook his head. "I can't imagine why the stable boy would allow that—even he should know better."

It took Jo a moment to figure out who the stable boy was. Her temper flared. "Luke is not a stable boy. He helps Aunt Viv because she needs it."

Mary Anne laughed. "Everyone around here knows Luke needs the money."

"So? What's wrong with earning money?"

"Nothing, I suppose." Mary Anne said as she studied a manicured nail.

"Maybe he's saving for college."

"College? Why would he want to go to college?" Tim asked.

"Why not?" Jo retorted.

Tim looked bewildered for a moment. "Well, his...*kind* don't go to college."

"His kind?" Jo felt white-hot anger sweep over her. "Do you mean—"

"Jo!" Wendy yelled from upstairs. "Can you come here for a minute?"

Rescued just in time. If she had stayed one more minute, Jo would have screamed at Tim and told him just what she thought. And Aunt Viv could send her packing if she made that kind of trouble with their relatives. Still, she was so mad she shook. She forced herself to walk slowly toward the door.

"So what's this about saddles?" Mary Anne asked Tim again.

"I'm buying Jo—and Wendy—English saddles."

Mary Anne's eyes narrowed and she looked at Jo. "You asked for a new saddle?"

"No! I…I did not."

"It's just a gift," Tim said.

Her cousin's eyes narrowed further.

"Jo!" Wendy yelled again.

"Coming!" Jo shouted back to Wendy and ran up the stairs.

Too late, she remembered she'd left the bottle of cologne on the table where Mary Anne would see it.

That was trouble Jo didn't need.

****

The bottle wasn't on the end table when Jo came down to supper later. Any hope that Mary Anne hadn't seen it was dashed when Mary Anne glared at her from across the table. Since Aunt Viv was seated there as well, Mary Anne didn't say anything, but Jo could feel waves of anger radiating off her cousin.

Even Wendy noticed. "What happened between you and Mary Anne?" she asked later when they had gone upstairs to Jo's bedroom and she was curled up on Jo's bed. "Mary Anne was shooting daggers at you."

For some reason, Jo felt reluctant to mention the perfume. First of all, Wendy hadn't gotten any, but Jo didn't want Wendy thinking she'd done anything to encourage Tim or—worse—teasing her about it.

"Mary Anne went to wash off your mom's perfume and put on some that Tim brought her. She heard him talking about the new saddles when she came back."

Wendy wrinkled her forehead. "So? His dad can afford it."

"That's not it," Jo replied, wondering how she should explain. "Tim said it was a gift and I don't think

61

Mary Anne liked the idea."

"Phooey. It's not like she and Tim are going steady or anything. I haven't even heard him call her his girlfriend since he's been back. He comes over here in the afternoons only because Mom won't let her go out at night."

Jo hadn't paid much attention to that fact, but she remembered now about Mary Anne meeting Bob. "Um…I think I saw Mary Anne leaving the other night."

Wendy bolted upright. "What?"

"It was pretty late—close to midnight. Your mom was already asleep. I went to the window to look at the full moon and saw Mary Anne outside." Jo paused. "Maybe she was just taking a walk."

"That late? I'll bet she was meeting someone." Wendy frowned. "Did you see anyone else or hear anything?"

"Um…well, I thought I heard a car down the road."

"Oh, my gosh!" Wendy's eyes grew round. "I'll bet it was Bob. Mary Anne will be so grounded!"

"I…I couldn't be *sure* it was Bob. Or even if Mary Anne got into the car."

"Why else would she take a walk at midnight? Just wait until I tell Mom!"

Jo winced. "Maybe it would be better not to say anything right now. I mean, your sister is already mad at me."

"That's stupid. Why should she be jealous about saddles? I'm getting one too."

"Maybe that doesn't matter to her."

"So what? Like I said, they're not steadies. Especially if Mary Anne is sneaking off to see Bob too."

"I can't be sure about that. Maybe we should just

wait and see if she does it again before telling your mom. I don't want Mary Anne to get even madder at me."

Wendy considered. "Well, she can be mean when she's mad. I guess it wouldn't hurt to wait until she cools down."

Jo breathed a sigh of relief. "If we catch her doing it again, we'll both tell your mom. Okay?"

"Okay." Wendy got up to leave. "But don't worry about the saddles. Once Mary Anne realizes they're just practical gifts, she'll get over it."

"I hope so," Jo said, but it was the bottle of perfume she worried about.

****

The saddles arrived a week later. So did Tim, since he was the one who brought them over. "Dad told them to rush the order." Tim placed both saddles atop the paddock fence.

"He didn't need to do that," Jo answered, knowing it cost more. "We could have waited a few more days."

"Yeah, we would have been okay," Wendy added.

Tim glanced at Luke, who had just come out of the barn. "Well, I didn't want the horses being risked by jumping with heavy Western saddles."

Jo knew that remark was aimed at Luke, but he ignored it. Instead, he ran his hand lightly over the soft leather of the padded flat seat. "Very nice."

"Of course," Tim answered and looped two new bridles over the fence as well. "No sense buying anything that isn't quality."

Luke nodded, apparently refusing to be baited. "Well, ladies, do you want to try them out?"

"Yes!" Jo and Wendy replied in unison and scampered off toward the barn. A few minutes later, they led their horses out.

"The first thing you need to do is get rid of those bridles," Tim said. "They have the wrong bit."

Luke shook his head. "These horses are trained for the curb bit, not a snaffle."

"In England they're trained to accept both bits," Tim replied.

"These aren't English horses," Jo said, remembering her first attempt at trying to "steer" Flame with the reins. "They're used to neck-reining. Like Luke said, they're used to the curb bit. Why confuse them?"

"Because if you want to compete in horse shows, you need to know how to ride properly. English style."

"What if we want to ride just for fun?" Wendy asked.

Tim looked at her as though she'd started speaking a foreign language. "Why bother to ride if you can't compete...and win?"

"But we don't have horse shows around here," Wendy said, "unless you mean the County Fair...and that's Western riding."

Tim sighed. "Just put on the proper bridles."

"No." Luke gathered both bridles in his hand. "Not yet. Let the horses get used to the feel of a different saddle first." He turned and walked into the barn, not waiting for Tim to reply.

"Impertinent farmhand," Tim muttered.

Jo didn't know what "impertinent" meant, but she didn't like Tim's calling Luke a farmhand in that tone of voice. She opened her mouth to retort, but before she could say anything, Wendy interrupted.

"Let's try out the saddles, okay?"

Jo clamped her mouth shut, reminding herself she

was a guest here. And the saddles were a gift. Her own mom would scold her for not being polite.

"Yes, let's. And we should really say 'thank you' to Tim," she added. "It really was generous of your dad to buy these."

"Not a problem. Here, let me saddle Flame for you."

"I can do it." Jo moved quickly to pick one of the saddles off the rail, thankful it was much lighter in weight than the Western one and she wouldn't be staggering with it. "Aunt Viv taught me how."

"Right, then," Tim said and helped Wendy with hers. They were just finished tightening the girths when Luke returned.

"Here." He moved toward Jo as she looked around for a mounting block. "Let me give you a leg up."

"Thanks." Jo put her boot into Luke's clasped hands and practically flew into the saddle as he lifted her with ease. That odd tingling sensation flashed through her again, even though she knew she couldn't feel anything through the sole of her boot. To hide her confusion, she busied herself with placing her feet in the stirrups and gathering the reins. Luke turned to help Wendy and Jo wondered again if he liked her cousin like a girlfriend. Wendy sure looked pleased.

Tim glowered at Luke. "Don't you have something else you should be doing? I'll take over here and teach the girls how to sit properly in an English saddle."

At that point, Jo had enough. She had forced herself to be quiet and not argue with Wendy's cousin, but she didn't want Tim "teaching" her about sitting in English saddles. She'd had a few lessons in New York, so she lowered her heels, the balls of her feet resting on the thin stirrup metal and shifted her weight forward, sitting straighter. Jo kept her hands low over the withers, although she held the reins in one hand so as not to confuse Flame, and nudged the mare forward into a slow trot. They posted in a circle. When she faced the front of the paddock again, Wendy and Tim were gaping at her, but Luke was nowhere to be seen.

****

Luke must have gone home, Jo realized a couple of hours later when she and Wendy brought their horses into the barn to unsaddle and brush down. The stall Silver Chief used was empty. "I guess Luke left?"

Wendy nodded. "He said earlier he had to help his dad."

Jo wondered about that. She knew the peas were ready for picking, since Aunt Viv had told her they were usually harvested in early August but spring planting had come a little early this year. The corn was growing tall, too, and soon would be ready to be detasseled, according to Wendy, who said kids worked the fields for extra money. Still, Luke had stayed away from Aunt Viv's place since the twins returned.

"I guess there's a lot to do on a farm," Jo said as she unbuckled Flame's girth.

"Especially in the summer," Wendy replied, "and Luke's dad is renting part of our acreage, so that's an extra load."

"His dad sounds pretty hardworking," Jo added as she took the saddle into the tack room and returned to lead Flame into her stall.

"Oh, he is. The reason you didn't meet him on the Fourth of July was because he was in the fields."

It occurred to Jo that she hadn't met Luke's mother, either, even though it seemed like every soul in town had been at the lake. "What about Luke's mom?"

Wendy paused in taking Jupiter into his stall. "She died when Luke was nine."

"Oh, my goodness!" Jo felt shock run through her. "I didn't know. What happened to her?"

"Mom said she was expecting a baby, and when she went to the hospital, something went wrong."

"How horrible!" Jo couldn't imagine losing one of her parents so young, but then, Wendy's dad had died just a couple of years ago, too. "Did the baby survive?"

Wendy shook her head. "She died."

"You mean like the Kennedy's baby last week?"

"No. The baby never lived. It was still-…stillborn. I was just seven when it happened, and I remember Mom saying Luke really took it hard."

"I'm sure. How terrible to have something like that happen. Does Luke have other brothers and sisters?"

"No. Just him and his dad." Wendy gave Jo a sharp look. "Why are you so interested in Luke?"

"I…I…" Jo remembered Wendy had hinted about being his girlfriend. "I… He just seems really nice, that's all. Nicer than Tim," Jo blurted out before she could stop herself. "I mean—"

"Tim can be stuck-up," Wendy agreed, "not at all like Tommy." She then proceeded to tell Jo about the practical jokes Tommy played on Tim and on everyone else, as well.

Jo listened as she groomed Flame's coat. At least, Wendy's thoughts had been diverted from Jo's questions about Luke. She was going to have to be careful not to ask too many questions in the future.

She finished brushing the mare and was headed toward the tack room when she noticed an envelope lying just inside the door of the stall. Part of it was covered with straw. Jo bent to pick it up, wondering who would have dropped it inside the barn. Turning it over, she took out a single piece of paper and felt her eyes widen as she read it.

Jo,

Can you meet me at the hidden cabin around seven o'clock tonight? I'd like to talk to you.

Luke

Jo stuffed the envelope in the pocket of her jeans, her fingers trembling with excitement. It didn't get dark until nearly eight o'clock and she remembered the way to the cabin. Luke wanted to talk to her! In private!

She could hardly wait for evening.

Chapter Seven

Jo slipped out the kitchen door after supper and stayed close to the shadows of the wall as she made her way to the trees behind the house. She hated having fibbed about her stomach being upset and wanting to go to her room to lie down, but she didn't know any other way to get out of the evening board games they usually played. Wendy had looked surprised, since *Gunsmoke* was on TV tonight and she knew Jo thought the deputy on that show was really cute. Jo sighed. Although there was some truth to her fib—her stomach was in knots—she still felt guilty.

Under the cover of the trees, the light dimmed considerably. She knew it was due to the dense foliage, but the stillness felt eerie. Jo forced herself to laugh out loud, a little surprised at how muffled the sound was. She wasn't going to be afraid of the woods. The "wolf" that had scared her last time had only been Wendy tricking her. Besides, she had at least an hour and a half of daylight left before real darkness descended…and Luke would make sure she got back safely.

Jo found the trail she and Wendy had used. It was pretty easy to follow here, but she knew it twisted and turned later. She sure didn't want to wind up at the old bridge. Even if it wasn't haunted, Jo had a funny feeling about the place when Luke took them there before. Even the horses hadn't wanted to get too close.

She wished she'd been able to take Flame tonight. She would have felt safer on the mare's back, but that would have meant taking the road for part of the way. Besides, she could hardly have ridden out of the stable without being noticed.

Breathing a sigh of relief when she arrived at the little clearing, Jo hurried around the cluster of trees to the cabin. Disappointment swept through her when she didn't see Silver Chief in the lean-to, but maybe Luke had walked. His place was only a mile from here. Jo approached the cabin, noting the door had been put back on its hinges and the firewood picked up. Had Luke come early to fix things?

Sweeping leaves off her shirt, Jo opened the door and stepped inside, feeling another wave of disappointment at finding the place empty. Maybe she was early. She wished she'd brought her Timex, but she wasn't used to wearing a wristwatch and had worn it only on the bus.

Well, whatever. Luke probably had to finish chores at his place and would get here soon. She really wasn't scared to be at the cabin alone. She wasn't. There were no wolves. She hadn't seen any other wild animals, either, unless she counted the occasional deer that showed up in the cornfield across the road or the cottontails that got into Aunt Viv's garden. Jo laughed again, the sound reassuring in the quiet. Deer and rabbits were hardly dangerous creatures.

She decided to sit down and wait. The single chair was actually pretty comfortable, and Jo leaned back dreamily. What did Luke want to talk to her about? Excitement churned in her stomach, loosing what felt like a dozen butterflies fluttering their wings. Was he going to tell her he hadn't been coming around because of Tim? Or maybe Luke wanted to talk about Wendy?

The butterflies landed with a thump in the pit of her stomach. Jo opened her eyes and looked around the cabin again. The table she'd dragged across the room had been put back in its place, and the hearth she'd hidden in now held half-burned logs. Someone had used this place. Did Luke come here often? Had he met Wendy here? The lump in Jo's stomach grew heavier. Had she been acting too friendly with Luke? Maybe he thought she was flirting with him? Maybe he wanted to tell her that Wendy was his girlfriend? Luke was polite enough to tell Jo something like that in private.

Suddenly, she wasn't sure if she wanted to talk to him.

Lost as she was in her dilemma, Jo looked out the window sometime later, realizing it had grown much darker while she was inside the cabin. Another dose of reality followed the first. Luke wasn't coming. Then why had he left her the note?

Geez. She was going to have to hurry to get back before the twilight faded into night, or she'd end up lost in the woods for sure. Jo set out at a jog, praying she'd pick up the right trail. She remembered zig-zagging to get here. As long as she didn't veer toward the river…

Her breath was ragged by the time she finally saw the lights of the farmhouse shining through the trees. Slowing to a walk, Jo tried to catch her breath as she crossed the lawn toward the back door, aware now that her legs were shaking. At least she'd made it back in one piece.

Jo stopped abruptly once inside the kitchen. Aunt Viv was reaching for her jacket on a hook by the door.

Mary Anne and Wendy were in the doorway, staring at Jo. Her aunt stepped back and folded her arms across her chest. "You have some explaining to do, young lady."

Jo swallowed hard. She couldn't say she'd been planning to meet Luke. "I…I was feeling better so I went for a walk—"

"Mary Anne said she saw you leave at six-thirty." Her aunt looked at the kitchen clock. "That was two-and-a-half hours ago."

Jo glanced in Mary Anne's direction. Her cousin had been in the parlor when Jo left. There was no way she could have seen Jo leaving through the back door.

Mary Anne smiled sweetly at her.

Jo felt like a bucket of cold water had sloshed over her. Mary Anne must have written the note to get her into trouble. The water turned to ice. *She* was the one who had told Wendy not to tattle on *Mary Anne*. Mary Anne had been the one who snuck out to meet Bob.

And then Jo felt her face flame with the heat of embarrassment. Hadn't she just done the same thing? Snuck out to meet a boy? What had she been thinking?

****

Aunt Viv confined Jo to her room for two days, bringing food to her room and allowing her out only to use the bathroom down the hall. Jo knew her aunt had gotten worried and was about to go out looking for her, just as she'd gotten back. Aunt Viv had believed the story that Jo had walked too far and gotten lost, although Wendy had given her a quizzical look. Jo accepted the punishment meekly, knowing it could have been a lot worse if her aunt knew she had gone out chasing after a boy. Even if that boy had been Luke. And her aunt would probably let her parents know, and Jo didn't even want to think about the grounding she'd get when they returned from Columbia.

Still, it felt wonderful to be outdoors again on the morning she regained her freedom. The past two days she'd watched Wendy riding Jupiter in the paddock, practicing jumps. Sometimes Luke would be there, but he usually left when Tim arrived. What surprised Jo was Mary Anne hanging around the paddock, but maybe she wanted to be near Tim.

Her cousins and aunt, as well as Luke, were in the kitchen when she went down for breakfast. From the delicious smell drifting into the hallway, she guessed Aunt Viv had made pancakes. It wasn't even Sunday, which meant—at least so she thought—it was her aunt's way of letting Jo know all was now well.

"Hi, everyone!" she said as she sat down. Mary Anne had a smirk on her face, but Jo decided to ignore it. She turned to Wendy. "I saw you practicing in the paddock. You're getting really good."

"Thanks. Luke helped."

"I know. I watched." Jo smiled at Luke. "You really are good with horses."

He shrugged and helped himself to another pancake.

Luke was so un-uppity. Jo was sure if she'd said the same thing to Tim he would have started bragging.

"I really mean it, Luke. I've seen how you handle Silver Chief, and you've helped me a lot, too."

"It's nothing," he replied, reaching for the pitcher of orange juice.

Jo frowned. Why was Luke not talking more? Or looking at her? A thought came to her. Had Luke written the note after all? And then decided to stand her up? Or lost his nerve? Maybe he was just embarrassed. She could hardly ask him about it here at the table.

Luke drained his juice, picked up his plate, and took his dishes and silverware to the sink. "I'll work on your tool shed this morning, ma'am."

"That will be fine, Luke," Aunt Viv said, "and I'll make a nice lunch before you go home."

He smiled at her aunt. "Thanks. That would be great."

Her aunt nodded, her smile remaining after he left. "Bless that boy. He didn't even slam the screen door."

Jo took her own dishes to the sink. Luke was definitely polite. And good at fixing things, if he was going to work on the tool shed. She thought about the replaced door on the cabin. Probably Luke's handiwork. Maybe she could mention she'd gone over there and noticed it. Maybe then he'd say something about the note.

She'd do that later. Right now what she really wanted to do was go for a long ride down the country roads and enjoy the sunshine and fresh air. Turning to ask Wendy if she wanted to go, Jo realized her cousin had already left the room. Well, no matter. A ride by herself would be just fine.

Taking some apple slices off a plate, Jo made her way to the stable. Flame nickered a greeting, daintily nuzzling the treats off Jo's palm when she entered the stall and closed the half-door behind her. Before she went for her ride, she decided she'd give the mare a good brushing. Flame deserved it, not having had attention for three days.

She had nearly finished her grooming when she heard footsteps outside and then Wendy's voice, followed by Luke's. Jo stilled when she heard her name mentioned.

"I don't think Jo likes Tim all that much," Wendy said as she opened Jupiter's stall to lead him out.

"Then why would she ask him to meet her at the cabin?" Luke asked.

Jo nearly dropped her brush. *What*? She stepped back into the shadows. She could hear Wendy pause.

"The cabin?" her cousin asked. "Jo said she got lost in the woods. What makes you think she went to the cabin?"

Silence seemed to hang in the air. Jo could scarcely breathe.

Luke finally spoke. "Mary Anne told me she did."

"Mary Anne told Mom that Jo went out. She didn't say anything about going to the cabin. I'd be surprised if she even remembered how to get there."

Another period of silence. Jo's heart was hammering so loudly she was sure they'd hear it any second. Thankfully, Wendy had resumed saddling her horse.

"Mary Anne didn't know about it until Tim told her the next day," Luke said. "She even showed me the note Jo wrote to Tim."

Jo suddenly felt lightheaded and leaned against the wall of the stall. What in the world was going on?

Wendy's voice sounded suspicious. "Let me see."

"I don't have it. Mary Anne kept it. She said it was pretty lowdown of Jo to try to steal her boyfriend. Then she started crying and ran away."

"It seems odd," Wendy said as she led Jupiter out of the barn. "I know Tim's been flirting with Jo, but I didn't think…"

Her voice faded away, and Jo didn't hear Luke's reply. As shaken as she was, she slid down the wall to the floor and hugged her knees.

Lies. Everything Mary Anne said had been a lie. But how could Jo prove it? She couldn't very well say she'd been hiding in the stall and listening.

What in the world was she going to do?

****

Luke didn't come into the farmhouse for breakfast the next morning. By the time she finished doing the dishes and went outside, he was hard at work stripping paint off the tool shed while Wendy picked weeds in the garden nearby.

Jo joined her, wondering if Luke would notice, but he didn't glance their way. She sighed as she knelt by the sprawling melon vines. The black earth felt warm against her bare knees. She was glad she'd worn culottes instead of jeans, even though she'd get as dirty as a little kid. The rough texture of the large leaves contrasted with the fine grains of soil as she slipped her hand beneath the vines to pluck the small blades of new weeds sprouting.

The vegetable garden had been a foreign place to her when she'd arrived in June. The row houses and brownstones in New York didn't have them. Those privileged enough to have a tiny plot of land no bigger than her aunt's cabbage patch "gardened" in pots and hanging containers on metal stands.

Wendy looked up from clearing weeds out of the strawberries and grinned. "At least now you can identify what is a weed and what isn't."

"It's pretty easy to do with melons," Jo retorted, although secretly she was proud of her acquired knowledge. The first time she attempted to help, she'd pulled out several eggplants before Aunt Viv stopped her. Of course, they were just tiny little sprigs in June, barely poking up, but she'd been mortified, just the same.

"Mom said she wanted some green beans for tonight," Wendy said.

"Sure, I'll pick them." Jo retrieved one of the containers Wendy had set down by the edge of the garden. Helping her aunt with the beans was one of Jo's favorite things to do. She liked snapping them.

In this instance, the beans happened to be on the other side of the garden, which meant she had to walk past Luke. Keeping him in her peripheral vision as she went past, Jo noticed he glanced in her direction. She turned her head to give him a smile, but he'd already looked away.

It hurt to think he thought she had asked Tim to meet her at the cabin. She didn't even like Tim very much, although Luke would have no way on knowing that since he seemed to make himself scarce whenever Tim was around.

Lunch was only marginally better. Since Luke was working on the tool shed all day, he came in to eat with the rest of them. Mary Anne announced, with a self-satisfied smirk, that Tim would be coming over to see her this afternoon. Luke gave Jo a quick look and then turned his attention back to the Hot Dish Aunt Viv had made.

"It's good Tim's coming over," Jo said. The comment earned her another look from Luke, this one more observant and Jo smiled weakly. "I mean...it's nice. For Mary Anne." Words kept trickling out of Jo's mouth like she couldn't stop them. "That Mary Anne has company."

"You're talking all weird," Wendy said.

Jo felt her face heat and turned her attention to the casserole. Normally, she liked the spicy-yet-sweet flavor Aunt Viv achieved by adding chili powder and raw sugar to the tomato sauce, but Jo suddenly had no appetite. She wished she could just tell Luke the rumor Mary Anne had started was a lie, but she didn't know how.

Maybe she should talk to Wendy, even if it meant confessing she'd been hiding in the stall listening.

Jo was still undecided when she went out to the barn after lunch. This time she left the stall door open while she brushed Flame. At least, no one would accuse her of hiding if someone came in.

She'd just finished picking Flame's hooves when she heard footsteps, too heavy to be Wendy's. Was Luke coming to the barn? Jo laid the hoof pick on a shelf and stepped outside the stall.

"I thought you might be in here," Tim said as he walked inside.

The one person she didn't want to see. "What...what do you want?"

One of his eyebrows lifted beneath his fringe of bangs as he came over to her. "I just wanted to say hi. I haven't seen you in a few days. Mary Anne told me about your being caught going to that old cabin in the woods."

"I can explain that!"

"You can?"

"I didn't write that note."

Tim gave her a quizzical look. "Note?"

"Yeah...where I was supposed to meet you."

"At the cabin?"

"Yes. I mean, no. That is—"

Tim stepped closer. "I'll be glad to meet you at the

cabin. When?"

"I…" Jo stopped at the sound of more footsteps. Her skin prickled as she craned her neck to look over Tim's shoulder just in time to see Luke spin around and walk away.

Chapter Eight

She had the absolute worst luck of anyone she knew. Jo's eyes still stung with unshed tears when she recalled the fiasco in the barn two days ago. She wasn't sure how much Luke had heard—she knew it must have sounded like she and Tim were making arrangements to meet at the cabin—but they hadn't spoken loudly because Tim had been standing so close that it looked like he was going to hold her or maybe even kiss her.

That didn't happen, since Jo had slipped past him, but Luke was already gone. He finished painting the shed that day, and she hadn't seen him since.

And now...*now* she was going to have to face Luke at the party Aunt Viv was having for Wendy's thirteenth birthday. Jo stood for a minute in the hallway and forced herself to take a deep breath before heading into the parlor.

Chairs and sofa had been pushed to the side and the carpet rolled up, exposing a hard oak floor perfect for dancing. Already several couples, including Mary Anne and Tim, were moving to the beat of "El Watusi" blaring from the hi-fi. Others were crowded around the card table in one corner that Aunt Viv had loaded with sandwiches, chips, dips, and soft drinks. Wendy was by the table talking to a couple of girls Jo had met at the Fourth picnic, but Jo didn't see Luke.

When Tommy approached her, Jo startled. He'd

combed his hair down on his forehead and she almost mistook him for Tim before remembering Tim was on the dance floor. They were also dressed the same. "What's with the clothes and the change in hair style?"

"We got a letter from Sean. He said the Beatles are really getting popular over there. Mary Anne thought it would be cute if Tim and I wore our hair the same today." Tommy laughed. "Tim and I used to really have fun with the 'twin' stuff." He took a sip of his cream soda and then belatedly handed Jo a lemon-lime soda pop. "Here. I don't know how you girls can drink that diet stuff, but Wendy said you liked it."

"Thanks." Jo accepted the bottle. "My mom doesn't like for me to eat a lot of sugar."

He raised a brow. "No birthday cake, then? Can I have your slice?"

"I don't think I can turn down cake." Jo smiled, thinking Tommy was so much more likable than Tim, even if he did like to play practical jokes. Not that he'd played any on her…yet. As a precaution, she sniffed her drink before taking a sip. Wendy had told her he once put black pepper in her soda pop.

The music changed to "Slow Twistin'" and Tommy took her drink and set it on a small table along with his. "Come on, let's dance."

"I don't really know how—"

"It's easy." He tugged at her hand, pulling her into the crowd. "You just move your hips, but do it slow."

The dance looked a little naughty to her, but bunches of the other kids were doing it, so Jo mimicked their moves. She noticed Mary Anne had gotten so close to Tim their hips were actually touching. She felt her eyes widen in shock and then grew bigger when Mary Anne took Tim's hand and led him out the front door into the dark night. Jo had a feeling they weren't headed for the swing on the porch. She looked around for Aunt Viv, wondering if she should go find her, and then the thought flew from her mind.

Luke stood by the doorway leading in from the kitchen. Silhouetted by the ceiling light in the hall, Jo could make out the angular planes of his face, although his eyes were shadowed. Dressed in a dark shirt and pants, his hair glistening raven-blue, he looked more like Ben Casey than a teenager.

He moved into the room. For a moment, his gaze met hers and then his eyes flicked to Tommy and he turned away.

Why… *Oh, no*. Jo almost groaned aloud. Luke had mistaken Tommy for Tim. Well, enough was enough. "Come on." Jo took Tommy by the hand and led him to the food table where Luke was now talking to Wendy. "I'm thirsty."

Tommy pointed. "But we have drinks over there."

"I'm hungry, too."

Luke glanced at Jo's hand as they approached and she realized she was still hanging onto Tommy. How stupid could she be? Quickly she let go.

"Happy Birthday," she said to Wendy and then added brightly. "How do you like Tommy's new hairstyle?"

"Actually, I'm Tim."

Jo rounded on him. "You're Tommy."

He smiled. "No, angel-face. I'm Tim."

"You aren't! Tim went outside with Mary Anne. I saw them." Jo looked at Luke, but his hazel eyes were cool and appraising. He gestured. "Mary Anne's over there."

Jo felt her blood chill as she slowly turned. Sure enough, her cousin had come inside and stood talking to a boy Jo didn't know. Mary Anne's face was flushed and her eyes bright. She seemed a little breathless, but nothing that couldn't be attributed to the song that had just finished playing. Jo surveyed the room. Where was Tim? Almost as though she had conjured him, he came through the front door seconds later. Jo gasped, her stomach burning as though she'd swallowed hot coals.

Tim had brushed his hair back like Tommy usually did.

Jo's head began to spin. The twins were playing a practical joke. A very unfunny one. She looked at Mary Anne, who smiled at her from across the room. Jo suddenly felt nauseous.

Just then, "Blue Velvet" came on and Wendy took Luke's hand. "You promised to dance with me."

"Yes, I did." Luke gave Jo a quick glance and then moved away. Jo blinked back tears. That was one of her favorite songs, and Luke was dancing it with Wendy.

"Are you crying?" Tommy asked.

"No." Jo shook her head quickly, even as a big tear trickled down. She stepped away from him.

He grabbed her arm. "Are you mad at me?"

"No." Jo shook loose and wiped her cheek with the back of her hand.

"Ah, geez. It was only a joke."

"Just leave me alone."

"But…" Tommy stopped and his eyes widened. "You like Luke, don't you?"

"No!" Jo turned and ran toward the hall. She raced up the stairs and into her room, not bothering to turn on the light. As she leaned against the door, strains of "It's My Party" drifted up the stairs.

It wasn't her party. It never had been.

Never.

Jo let the tears flow.

****

Jo looked in the mirror the next morning before going down to breakfast. At least her eyes weren't rimmed in red and the puffiness had gone down. She didn't want anyone—especially not Luke, if he joined them this morning—knowing she'd spent half the night crying. She would just pretend everything was fine. The heroines in her favorite movies, *Where the Boys Are* and the *Gidget* movies always had problems, but they never failed to keep their heads held high. She would be like them!

She marched down the steps, hesitating for only a second in the hallway before forcing a smile onto her face and entering the kitchen.

Thankfully, Luke wasn't there. Jo hadn't realized her knees were shaking until she sat down on the nice, solid chair.

"You left the party early," Aunt Viv said as she set a glass of orange juice down for Jo. "Were you not feeling well?"

"Um…my stomach was a little upset."

Aunt Viv frowned. "Something you ate?"

"I…I'm not sure." She'd felt sick to her stomach, but not from food.

"Do you feel better this morning? Maybe I should take your temperature."

"No. I'll be fine." Jo thought of her movie examples and put the smile back on her face. "Really. Probably just a little bug."

"Are you sure?" Mary Anne sounded solicitous. "Tommy said you looked kind of green."

Did Mary Anne mean green with jealousy? Had Tommy said something? It was bad enough that Tommy guessed she liked Luke. She didn't want the whole world knowing how stupid she was.

Wendy started to giggle. "Wasn't it funny how Tim and Tommy pretended to be each other?"

Aware that Mary Anne watched her, Jo nodded. "They sure fooled me." Jo thought they'd fooled Luke, too, but that didn't matter. Not anymore. She blinked rapidly to keep tears from forming again.

"Yeah," Wendy agreed. "They used to do that all the time. It drove their teachers crazy. They spent a lot of time in seventh grade in the principal's office."

"Which is probably why their father sent them off to England last year." Aunt Viv put a bowl of cinnamon oatmeal in front of Jo. "Now eat this, dear. It'll settle your stomach."

"Thank you." Jo managed to swallow a few spoonsful, even though her stomach threatened to lurch into her mouth at any moment.

"It got funnier after you left," Wendy said. "Tommy pushed his hair back like he always wears it, but Tim left his back too. Then they both started claiming to be Tommy. Pretty soon, lots of people were confused."

Jo wondered if Luke had figured out it was really Tommy she'd been talking to and not Tim, but she couldn't ask.

Mary Anne smiled. "Luke turned out to be a good dancer, didn't he, Wendy?"

"Oh, yes! He didn't even step on my toes once. And

I loved the slow dancing."

Jo put down her spoon. She didn't dare try to eat more. "I think maybe my tummy's still upset. May I be excused?"

"Of course, dear." Aunt Viv leaned over to feel her forehead. "You don't feel like you have a fever."

"I don't think I do." Jo stood. "I should be fine later."

"Well, I'll bring up some peppermint tea."

"Thanks." Jo turned to walk toward the stairs, forcing herself not to run.

"I hope you feel better," Mary Anne called after her.

Jo was pretty sure she didn't mean it.

****

"Why do people say mean things about people they don't even know?" Wendy asked several evenings later. They'd just watched the national news on TV and the commentators were going wild over a speech by a man named Martin Luther King, Jr. "I mean, what's wrong if he has a dream of all people being equal?"

"There is nothing at all wrong about dreaming, sweetie," Aunt Viv said to her. "The real problem is that some people still have to dream because they aren't treated equally, even nearly a hundred years after the Civil War was fought."

Mary Anne yawned. "Well, it's not our problem. We don't have any black people living anywhere close to us."

Her mother frowned at her. "It's everyone's problem, Mary Anne."

"There's a black professor in the history department at the university where my dad works. They're good friends," Jo added.

"I've only seen black people when I've gone to Minneapolis," Wendy said. "I've never talked to one."

"They're no different from you and me," Jo replied.

Aunt Viv nodded. "That's right. Don't you remember learning about the Civil War last year, Mary Anne?"

She blinked. "I guess."

Wendy rolled her eyes. "She was probably drooling over some boy."

"Was not!"

"Never mind that," Aunt Viv said firmly. "It's taught in the eighth grade, so Wendy and Jo will be studying it. Mary Anne, you can help with their homework, since you don't seem to remember the lessons."

Mary Anne's lower lip pushed out in a pout and Wendy giggled.

"I'm just glad I'll be going to school here," Jo said.

"So are we, dear."

She'd been so excited a couple of weeks ago when her parents had written saying more relics had been discovered and the dig was extended. Then her hopes at staying at the farm were dashed when another letter had followed saying her parents would send her to boarding school until they returned. Aunt Viv had hugged her and said she wouldn't hear of it.

"It'll be so exciting to be in the eighth grade!" Wendy said.

Mary Anne sniffed. "It's not *high* school."

Wendy stuck out her tongue. "You're not in *high* school yet either."

"I will be."

"Girls!" reprimanded their mother.

Jo quit listening to their protests. She was just glad she was staying…and she'd be near Luke.

****

With September approaching, harvest time was on them. Luke helped his father harvest the oats and bale hay, and then they moved on to help other nearby farmers. Aunt Viv explained that sharing expensive farm equipment like combines saved everyone money. She busied herself preparing "lunch"—really a midmorning meal of sandwiches and coffee and something sweet— for the men harvesting her fields. Jo had helped her take the food out to wherever the men were, foolishly hoping to see Luke, but he wasn't working Aunt Viv's acreage. Jo hadn't seen much of him since the party. She wondered if he was deliberately keeping away, although it really made no sense that he would.

However, harvest time kept Tim and Tommy away too, since they were given jobs at various farms stacking hay bales as they came in and feeding livestock while the farmers were in the fields. According to her aunt, timing was everything when it came to getting the crops in. One heavy rainstorm could ruin—or at least greatly reduce— production and that could reduce profits, something Jo had never thought about before.

She and Wendy were playing a game of Crazy Eights one evening when Mary Anne came into the parlor and dejectedly shuffled through the stack of 45s by the hi-fi. Sighing, she put on one of them and flounced onto the sofa. "Oh, Lord! Can life get any more boring than this?"

Wendy rolled her eyes. "Imagine being dateless on a Saturday night!"

Mary Anne glared at her. "You wouldn't know.

Everyone who lives in town is probably at the bakery right now."

"Well, you can't drive yet, and you don't want Mom showing up to get you, so it's your own fault you're home tonight."

The bakery was owned by a young couple who had moved from St. Paul last year, according to Wendy. They had been an immediate hit with teens when they decided to serve burgers and fries at night. Aunt Viv had taken them there once—early—and Mary Anne had refused to sit with them.

"Oh, shut up."

"You shut up. You're just mad because Tim hasn't come over."

Mary Anne sniffed. "He called, bird-brain. He and Tommy are just too tired after working all day long."

Jo wondered if that was the reason Luke hadn't come around either.

"Besides, if Mom would let me date Bob, I could be at the drive-in for the movie." Mary Anne heaved a dramatic sigh. "I think *The Birds* is showing."

"As if Mom would let you go to the drive-in, let alone with Bob."

"I saw that movie in New York," Jo said. "It's really scary. I wouldn't want to be sitting in a dark car watching it."

Mary Anne arched an eyebrow and smiled like a cat who'd found spilled cream. "Of course, *you* wouldn't."

Jo wasn't sure what she meant by that, but Wendy snorted. "If Mom ever caught you out with Bob, you'd be grounded for a year."

Mary Anne's expression changed to guarded speculation. "What do you mean?"

Wendy gave her a smug look. "Let's just say that you were seen out one night."

Her sister narrowed her eyes. "Who saw me?"

Wendy shrugged. "Maybe a little bird with a real brain. Anyway, it was late. And there was a car waiting at the end of the yard road."

"I didn't..." She stopped abruptly when Aunt Viv came into the room with a plate of warm cookies and flopped back against the couch, but her gaze turned on Jo.

Jo busied herself stacking the cards, wishing Wendy hadn't said anything. Mary Anne had already caused enough trouble for her—or at least, Jo thought she had. She really didn't need anything else to go wrong.

Especially not now when it seemed Luke was avoiding her. If only she knew if he were staying away because he was really tired or if it was because he thought she had asked Tim to meet her at the cabin. Luke had overheard part of the conversation that made it sound like she had. If only she could have had a chance to explain to Luke about the mix-up. But then, how would she even start? That she thought Luke had asked to meet her there? And that she'd gone, thinking he was there? He'd obviously not written the note, so she'd just be embarrassing herself. Plus, he would think she was the kind of girl who would sneak away to meet a boy. But then, didn't he already think that? Jo closed her eyes and rubbed her forehead. Why was life so hard?

"Do you have a headache?" Aunt Viv asked as she put the cookies on the coffee table. "Are you not feeling well?"

"No...I mean yes. I...I'm fine." Jo put her hand down. "My eyes just burned."

"Allergies? With all the grain being harvested, there's lot of dust in the air."

"That's probably it." Harvesting…maybe she could find out something about Luke, anyhow. "How much longer will the farmers be in the fields?"

"At least another week. They really need to take advantage of this good weather," her aunt replied. "Besides, school's starting in two weeks."

Would Luke stay away another week? When Mary Anne groaned, Jo was reminded that meant Tim and Tommy would be in the fields, too. Good for her, but her cousin's moodiness was just going to get worse. And she didn't want Mary Anne pulling any more tricks on her.

Well, she should be able to avoid Mary Anne. How hard could that be? Jo would just stay busy in the barn and help with the garden. It was only a few days, after all.

And, even if Luke stayed away that long, Jo would see him in a couple of weeks when school began. The middle school and high school were in the same building and they'd be riding the bus into town. She'd just have to figure out what to say to him.

****

"You got a letter!" Wendy exclaimed the next day as she came up from the mailbox at the end of the yard road.

Jo looked up from the sandwiches she was making for Aunt Viv to take to the men for lunch. "Is it from my parents?"

Wendy put the letter down on the table. "Yeah."

"Okay." Jo wrapped the sandwich in plastic and wiped her hands on the kitchen towel. She usually got a letter from Columbia every two weeks. The last she'd heard, her parents were excited over more ancient pottery found at the dig.

The first thing she noticed was that the envelope didn't have the familiar red and blue air-mail stripes around the edges. Jo picked it up and frowned. The postmark was New York. That was odd. She opened the letter and scanned her mother's neat handwriting, then swallowed hard, feeling like lead had just settled in her stomach.

"What is it, dear?" Aunt Viv asked.

"My mother is home."

"In New York? Your parents weren't going to be back until after Christmas."

"They weren't supposed to be home this soon." Jo glanced at the letter again. "Mom says she came down with jungle fever and the doctor said she needed to be in a different climate to recuperate."

"Your dad didn't come with her?" Wendy asked.

Jo shook her head. "He couldn't. He's in charge of the dig."

"Well, she's welcome to come out and stay with us until your dad gets back," Aunt Viv said. "We've got plenty of room."

"Thanks, but Mom says the fever really made her weak." Jo felt the sting of tears in her eyes as she held up a bus ticket. "She wants me to come home immediately. She needs me there."

Her aunt took a deep breath. "Then you must go."

"But what about school?" Wendy asked. "You can't go back to New York! We have all these plans for eighth grade!"

"Wendy, stop that. Jo's mother needs her right now," Aunt Viv said.

"But—" Wendy started to cry. "I don't want her to go!"

Jo didn't want to go, either. She'd miss the riding, and she didn't want to leave Flame. Even though the mare wasn't hers, she'd taken care of her all summer.

And Luke. Would she even have the chance to say goodbye?

Chapter Nine

"You want to play Crazy Eights?" Wendy asked Jo after supper that evening.

Jo looked at the pack of cards on the parlor table. "I guess." She didn't feel like playing cards or games. Her world had been turned upside down by her mother's letter. She knew she couldn't stay at the farm forever, but she'd thought she had until Christmas. Wendy promised they always had snow for Christmas and the small lake was perfect for ice skating. Aunt Viv added that the Johnsons, down the road, had a real horse sleigh and the local church choirs took turns caroling in it. Jo had been looking forward to that. Now she would be spending the holiday on the slushy streets of Brooklyn instead.

"How do you like this spirit shirt?" Mary Anne asked as she waltzed in, holding up a T-shirt with the high school's maroon-and-gold colors and logo. "I'm going to wear it the first day."

Jo tried not to be envious. She'd seen the shirts in the window of the local dime store, along with pom-poms and megaphones with "Eagles are #1" printed on them. Wendy had informed her that football rivalry was strong amongst the small towns in the area, especially those less than ten miles apart. Jo had planned to buy a shirt since Luke would be on the varsity team this year, but now she wouldn't need to.

Mary Anne selected a record from the stack and

turned on the hi-fi. The Beach Boys' "Be True To Your School" filled the room as she held the shirt against herself and began to dance. "High school is going to be so much fun!"

"Oh, for Pete's sake!" Wendy jumped off the couch and lifted the needle off the record. "Can't you find something else to play?"

Mary Anne slid her glance over to Jo before turning toward her sister with wide eyes. "What's wrong with that song?"

Wendy rolled her eyes. "You know very well Jo won't be going to our school."

"I didn't know our cousin was so sensitive." Mary Anne sighed dramatically. "Let me put something else on, then."

"Good." Wendy said as she went back to the sofa to pick up the cards.

"Is this better?" Mary Anne asked with an innocent smile as she changed the record to "He's So Fine."

"Yeah," Wendy muttered and began to deal.

Jo winced inwardly. The song reminded her of Luke. She didn't think Wendy had caught on that she had a crush on him, but Jo was pretty sure Mary Anne had. Why else would she be acting so mean?

But it really didn't matter how her cousin acted. Jo blinked fast to keep the tears away. Luke hadn't come over. She hadn't seen him on Aunt Viv's acreage when she took lunch out to the men, either. She'd even coerced Wendy into riding by his parents' farm, but Jo couldn't think of an excuse to actually go onto the place. At any rate, the yard had been empty when they rode by. Luke seemed to be avoiding her since the party.

And in two days, she would be leaving.

****

Jo set her suitcases down by the kitchen door. Thankfully, the room was empty. She didn't know if she could take her aunt's sympathetic looks or any more of Wendy's schemes for Jo to stay at the farm. They both knew those plots wouldn't work, and last night they'd cried well past midnight.

"Good morning," Aunt Viv said crisply as she entered the kitchen. "What would you like for breakfast?"

Her last breakfast on the farm. Jo swallowed hard. She didn't need to do any more crying. "I'm not hungry."

"Nonsense. You need to eat something."

Before you leave. Her aunt didn't say the words, but they lingered unspoken in the air. Lots of sentences the past two days had been left hanging. "Maybe just some cereal. Could I...do I...have enough time to go say goodbye to Flame?"

"Of course, dear."

Jo nodded and practically bolted out the kitchen door and across the yard to the barn, not caring that she was wearing a dress and white flats. Inside, the familiar smells of hay and leather and horse assailed her nose. She breathed in the welcoming aroma. Even if she got a chance to go riding in New York, it wouldn't be like this. She'd miss taking care of Flame—feeding her, brushing her, even cleaning the stalls and polishing the tack—but most of all, she'd miss riding the mare along winding country roads. The sounds of the country—songbirds in the trees, the river flowing over rocks, cows bawling in the distance, the soft plop of Flame's hooves in the loose gravel—all sounds she wouldn't hear in New York. The horses at the public stables would be strangers.

"You're my friend, aren't you?" Jo whispered as Flame stuck her head over the half-open door of her stall and nuzzled Jo's hand. She stroked the soft muzzle. "Sorry, girl. I forgot to bring an apple."

"Here."

Jo spun at the sound of Luke's voice. He stood in the doorway, dressed in blue jeans and a tight, white T-shirt, the sun highlighting the raven sheen to his hair. She had hoped—prayed—she'd see him before she left, but everyone had been working in the fields until dark to get the crops in. The weather people were forecasting thunderstorms and hail. And now that her prayers had been answered, she was strangely tongue-tied. "You're here."

Luke nodded and walked toward her. "I stopped by the house to say goodbye." He held out an apple. "Your aunt said you'd forgotten this."

"Thanks." That warm tingle shot up her arm again when her fingers brushed his as she took the apple. She felt her cheeks grow warm and kept her eyes on the fruit. "I felt really guilty about not giving Flame a last apple."

"I feel kinda guilty too."

Jo's gaze flashed to Luke's face. "Why?"

"For not coming over."

"You were working in the fields."

"I could have cleaned up and ridden over later."

Jo hesitated, not sure she should ask. "Why…didn't you?"

Color rose on his cheekbones. "When I heard you and Tim talking about meeting at the cabin, I thought—"

"I wasn't meeting him. I thought I was meeting you!" Jo clamped a hand over her mouth too late.

Luke stared at her. "Why would you think that?"

Jo turned toward Flame, feeding the mare the apple so she wouldn't have to look Luke in the eye. "I found a note with your signature—"

"*My* signature?"

Jo nodded, still not looking at him. "Mary Anne wrote it. At least, I think she did. I can't prove it."

"What did the note say?"

"You—it…the note—asked me to meet you at the cabin after supper."

Luke took her shoulder, turning her around. "I would never ask you to sneak out at night to meet me."

"I know." Jo's face felt on fire. She had to change the subject before she made a complete fool of herself. "Tim got a note, too, only it was supposed to be from me asking to meet him at the cabin. That's the conversation you overheard."

Luke dropped his hand, his hazel eyes growing dark. "It seems Mary Anne has been pulling all kinds of tricks. Tommy told me it was her idea for him and Tim to pretend to be each other at that party."

Jo nodded. "That's what I thought."

"But why?"

"She didn't want you to like me," Jo blurted out without thinking.

Luke frowned. "Why would she not want me to like you?"

"Oh, she doesn't care if you *like* me—"

"But you just said…" Luke stopped, looking puzzled. "You're a nice person. Why wouldn't I like you?"

A *nice* person. Jo did a silent prayer that somehow the floorboards in the barn would break apart and she'd fall through a big hole. A *nice* person. Luke thought she was *nice*. Luke didn't like her the way she liked him. *Please, God.* She just couldn't get any more embarrassed. Maybe it was a good thing she was leaving, after all.

"Jo?"

She realized Luke was waiting for an answer. Apparently, she *could* get more embarrassed since the floor remained solid beneath her feet. "I…uh…well…uh—"

"What are you trying to say?"

"I…there are just different kinds of like." Jo took a deep breath. "Mary Anne didn't want you to like me because she knew I liked you."

Luke blinked. "Huh?"

"It's all just silly. Never mind." Jo turned toward Flame, wishing she had some apple left. Then she felt Luke's hand on her shoulder again, turning her around.

"I don't get it."

Please God. The floor? When nothing happened, Jo sighed. Since she was leaving anyway, she might as well just tell Luke the truth. "Okay. I know I'm too young to date—not that you asked or anything—but I…*liked* you kinda like a boyfriend." She looked down at the floor. There. She'd said it.

Luke made a strangled sound and then his fingertips were under her chin, lifting it, causing her to look at him.

"I think I understand now," he said and then dipped his head, brushing his lips across hers in a soft, gentle kiss before he released her and stepped back.

The room spun. Jo felt the blood drain from her face and then quickly return like a spouting geyser of fire threatening to explode her skin. Her lips felt fuller and a strange sensation slid down her spine. She gasped as if she'd just run a mile.

Luke's eyes looked like molten gold as he smiled, his dimple showing. "I wish I'd known."

Jo wasn't sure she could speak coherently, but she was spared an answer when Wendy called her name, appearing at the doorway seconds later.

"Mom says it's time to go."

Jo nodded mutely, still not trusting her voice. She glanced at Luke.

"I'll take care of Flame for you," he said.

Jo hesitated and then nodded again, turning to follow Wendy out of the barn. Some goodbyes were just too hard.

****

Jo dared not look back as the bus lumbered away from the general store that served as the passenger depot in Middletown. Her aunt's eyes had been suspiciously bright as she hugged Jo. Wendy openly let tears stream down her face. Even Mary Anne had lost her usual smirk, although that might be because she was eager to see her friends at the corner drugstore. Thankfully, Luke had stayed behind. Jo didn't think she could have taken seeing him standing there, waving goodbye with the rest of them.

The bus picked up speed as it turned onto the open highway and headed southeast toward Chicago. Fields rushed by the windows, some of them with bales of hay waiting to be picked up, others with cornstalks still standing, but Jo hardly noticed. Each mile was taking her farther and farther away from a place she'd grown to love.

How ironic that the first song she heard when she

turned on her transistor was "Then He Kissed Me." The insides of her tummy felt all fluttery again, as though she'd swallowed a bunch of butterflies that suddenly left their perches. Not that she hadn't relived that short kiss a million times already. It had been her first kiss…and Luke had given it to her. Jo closed her eyes, her insides suddenly mushy as she recalled his fingers lifting her chin, then him bending down to brush her mouth with his…

"Are you all right, young lady?"

Jo snapped her eyes open to find a grandmotherly sort leaning across the aisle and looking at her with concern. "Yes. Why?"

"You whimpered and you had your eyes closed. I thought you might be in pain."

She felt her cheeks warm. She couldn't very well tell the lady that yes, she was in pain, but it wasn't the sort someone older would understand. "I guess maybe I was dozing off."

"Well, that's just fine then." The woman smiled and picked up the knitting she'd laid on her lap. "I just wanted to be sure you were all right."

Jo thanked her and turned off her radio as "Losing You" came on. She didn't need to be reminded. Not that she was actually sure what she had lost, since she'd never had a date with Luke. Still. He had kissed her. Did it mean as much to him as it did to her? Suddenly she felt like she'd swallowed a lump of coal instead of butterflies. Maybe the kiss didn't mean anything to him at all. Maybe—*please, no*—maybe he had done it because she had practically asked him to kiss her. Hadn't she? Jo's cheeks heated again. Maybe…maybe Luke was used to kissing girls. He was two years older and in high school already.

Her stomach churned, and Jo closed her eyes, leaning her head against the seat. Did it really matter why Luke had kissed her? There was no way to find out. She was going back to New York and he'd be in Minnesota. She wiped a tear away before the lady across the aisle could see it.

No matter what, Jo would remember that kiss forever. Slowly, she let the quiet clicking of the knitting needles lull her to sleep as the bus rolled on.

Chapter Ten

As Jo stepped off the bus at the Brooklyn station, she almost didn't recognize her mother. The thin, pale-faced woman quietly seated on a bench bore only a slight resemblance to the vibrant person Jo remembered. Three months ago, when her mom left for Columbia, she had been bouncy, full of energy, and fussing about losing ten pounds. Now she looked frail, a notion confirmed when her mother stood and teetered for a moment before getting her balance.

Jo rushed forward. "Mom! What are you doing here? You look horrible."

Her mother smiled wanly. "I wanted to be here to greet you. Give me a hug."

As Jo wrapped her arms around her, she could feel how slight a frame was beneath the heavy sweater. A sweater that should have been too hot for September. Her mother was trembling, too. "Come on, let's go home."

"That sounds good."

Jo picked up her suitcases and headed toward the Metro. "We'll be home soon."

"Let's take a taxi instead of the subway."

She almost dropped her luggage. Taxis were an expense her parents rarely indulged in. Living on college professors' salaries in New York made them stick to a tight budget. Her mom must be a lot sicker than Jo thought. "Sure."

It was somewhat of a minor miracle that they were able to find one. A silver-haired lady with a walking stick had summoned a cab and must have noticed how unsteady Jo's mother was because she offered to share her ride. Her mother muttered something about angels walking on this earth and Jo began to wonder if her mom's thinking had been affected as well.

Jo had forgotten how crowded the city was…and how loud. Hordes of people waited at street corners for lights to change, and when they did, it looked like twin armies advancing on each other. Horns honked continually, and tires squealed as drivers hit brakes to keep from colliding with the car in front of them. Their own cabbie laid on his horn as a truck ran a red light. The noise drowned out what Jo suspected was a string of curse words coming out of his mouth, and then she gasped as a motorcycle swerved around them. Its back wheel brushed the taxi's fender, causing the cab to veer right, barely avoiding scraping against the car beside it. The bike wobbled, the rider's boots scraping the pavement before he managed to right it. He throttled up and disappeared between two lanes of cars.

"Idiot!" the cabbie said and then glanced back. "Everyone all right?"

The silver-haired lady clutched the armrest and Jo's mother looked a bit shaken, but she managed to nod. Jo nodded too, thinking how close they had come to being in a wreck. This kind of thing wouldn't happen in Middletown, Minnesota. The heaviest traffic there was on Saturday nights when kids cruised the town square before going to the bakery or the drive-in movie. She and Wendy had observed those activities a couple of times when Aunt Viv had taken them to the local ice cream shop for a treat. And the teenagers drove so slowly that a lame dog could have outpaced them, since the point was to see and be seen as they went round and round the same block.

It seemed the cabbie was going round and round too. At first Jo thought maybe he'd mistaken them for tourists, since the silver-haired lady had given him the name of a nice hotel on Adams Street. It wasn't unheard of for cabbies to increase their fares by taking a longer route, but then Jo realized he had exited Flatbush Avenue to avoid the bumper-to-bumper, stand-still congestion where Atlantic and Fourth converged with it.

Still, she breathed a sigh of relief when the taxi pulled up in front of their walkup. As her mother paid their part of the fare, Jo carried her suitcases up the steps to their door and then watched as her mother used the railing for support. The uneasiness she'd felt when she first saw her mother increased. "How sick are you, Mom?"

"I'm recovering, sweetie. Don't worry."

As Jo followed her mother inside, shock rolled over her like a cold wave off Coney Island Beach. The small living room to her right was a mess, and through the open door to her left, Jo could see dishes stacked on the kitchen counter and pans sitting on the stove. Her mother had always been meticulous, with everything neat and orderly...a result of her occupation as an archeologist, her mother always laughingly teased.

Her mother wasn't laughing now. Instead, she'd sunk onto the sofa, covering herself with a blanket that had been tossed there. She shivered, looking exhausted. "Welcome home, sweetheart."

A sliver of fear sliced through Jo's stomach. Her

mother was much sicker than she was letting on. Jo looked around, wishing her father were here.

****

"You never want to do anything," Rosalie Matteo, Jo's best friend from seventh grade, complained as they took the bus home from middle school. "You need to have some fun!"

"You know Mom has been sick. I really haven't had time to hang out after school," Jo replied, a little irritated that Rosalie didn't understand. Rosie liked having lots of people around her and she got bored sitting at home.

"Yeah, I know, but it's been like two months already. Your mom looked pretty good last week when I came by."

"She's getting better. I just kinda want to stay close by, though."

"Well, okay, but in three weeks it'll be Thanksgiving—you're planning to come with me and my folks to see the tree lighting in Times Square, aren't you? Remember what fun we had last year?"

"Yes, it was fun." Jo remembered how excited she'd been. It had been her first time to see the big tree lit. The air had been crisp and cold, making it feel like the Christmas season, and the jostling crowds had been good-natured, reflecting the holiday spirit. Somehow, though, she wasn't that excited about it this year. After spending the summer in the quiet countryside, the crowds at the Square would seem rowdy, standing shoulder to shoulder and shouting at the tops of their lungs. And the subways would be packed getting there and getting back.

Rosalie glanced at her. "You don't sound very excited."

"I guess I've just been worried about my mom." Jo *had* been worried, especially the first couple of weeks when her mother seemed so weak. Her dad sounded even more worried when he called every few days. He'd tried to get someone else to take over the dig, but the Columbian government was holding his passport until they could verify he wasn't leaving with any relics.

Even as her mother got stronger and was pretty much out of danger, Jo still didn't feel an urge to get on a bus or train to go to the mall or a movie with her friends. But Rosie would think that weird. "Besides, everything is so crowded."

"Geez. Don't tell me you're still missing that hick town in Minnesota!"

Jo shrugged, not answering directly. She'd tried to explain to Rosalie and several others how peaceful and quiet the country had been. They'd shaken their heads in sympathy, which meant they didn't understand at all. When she told them about the town square, the roller-skating rink, and the bakery, they'd looked at her as though she'd come from a foreign country, so she'd stopped trying to explain.

But she missed it. Wendy wrote that an early frost had turned the tree leaves brilliant yellows, oranges and reds, and nearly everyone in town had decorated for Halloween with mini-haystacks and jack-o-lanterns on front porches, and how she'd taken some little kids trick-or-treating. Jo couldn't even imagine doing that in Brooklyn, especially after dark. And now, Middleton was preparing to celebrate Thanksgiving with the city council providing twenty turkeys, along with dressing, and the townspeople bringing the rest of the trimmings to the city auditorium for a midday feast. Aunt Viv was baking several pies to take. If they got a couple more freezes, the lake would be ready for ice skating afterwards.

"Mom and Dad want to go into town early to see where the World Trade Center is going to be built. Then maybe they'll let us shop at Macy's," Rosalie said. "I want to get some of those white designer go-go boots they have there."

"Sounds good." Jo would have preferred cowboy boots, although she didn't mention that. When she'd talked about riding Western-style, that had earned her dubious looks too. All she really wanted to do was go horseback riding, but in the city that was expensive. With her mother not being able to work, their budget was even tighter, so Jo didn't ask if she could go.

She missed Flame. She missed taking care of the mare and even missed the smells of the barn. If her mom hadn't gotten sick, Jo would still be there on the farm with Flame and Wendy and Luke…

"This is my stop," Rosalie said, breaking into Jo's reverie. "See ya tomorrow."

"Okay." Jo settled back on the bus seat. *Luke*. He'd sent her a postcard about a month ago, telling her Flame was fine and that the Eagles' football team had a chance at winning District. Jo had reread the short note so often that the ink was beginning to fade from her handling it. She'd finally put the card inside a dresser drawer, knowing it was silly to keep thinking about their kiss, especially when Luke hadn't mentioned it, but then, he wouldn't on a postcard. Maybe he'd send her a letter soon.

****

Jo fingered the letter in the pocket of her jacket as

she walked back to class after lunch. Rosalie gave her a curious look.

"What's in your pocket?"

Jo felt her cheeks warm even though the hallway was cool, thanks to someone having left the double doors at the end open, letting the cold north wind in along with a few flakes of snow. "Nothing."

"Right." Her friend snorted. "You've had your hand in that pocket all morning."

Jo dropped her hand to her side. "Have not."

"Have." Rosalie poked her. "Come on, give."

"It…it's just a letter from a friend." Putting it that way was something like saying the Beatles were just a bunch of English boys with funny haircuts. Luke had written! An honest-to-goodness letter, even if it was just one page. The Eagles were still undefeated in football, the horses were fine, and he'd enclosed a Polaroid of himself dressed as Conrad Birdie for the school's Halloween costume party. He kinda even looked like Conrad Birdie with his hair slicked back like that. Jo felt a ping of jealousy when she wondered if he'd kissed a girl like in the movie. But then, he hadn't mentioned any girls, and neither had Wendy when she'd written, so Jo decided he must not have. At any rate, Rosalie was right. She'd had her hand in her pocket during every class this morning. The envelope felt as soft as flannel by now.

Her friend stopped abruptly in the hallway and grabbed her arm. "Oh, my gosh! Is it from a boy?"

Jo almost choked. "What makes you think that?"

"The look on your face. You got all dreamy-eyed just like that." Rosalie clapped a hand to her mouth. "That's why you liked Minnesota! You have a boyfriend!"

She felt her face flame. "No. I mean...I don't think so. I...he's just someone I like. He's really good with horses."

"Horses, phooey! Did you go out with him?"

"No..." Thankfully the bell rang. "Come on, we're going to be late for Mr. Pascal's class. You know how mad he gets."

As they settled into their seats rather noisily, Jo knew Rosalie wanted to ask more questions, but Mr. Pascal was a real stickler about talking without permission.

He cleared his throat disapprovingly as he peered at them over the rim of the glasses perched on the edge of his nose and then finished taking roll. "All right, class. Just because it's the Friday before Thanksgiving week doesn't mean we have to be rowdy. We have work to do today." He opened his history book and then lifted one eyebrow as the class just sat there. He cleared his throat again and there was a rustle of sound as books scraped across desks and pages were flipped.

"Perhaps, Miss Thompson, you could enlighten us as to the circumstances that caused John Paul Jones to utter the words, 'I have not yet begun to fight.' Where was he at the time?"

Panic swept over Jo. She didn't remember much about last night's reading assignment. Luke's letter had been waiting when she got home from school and her mind hadn't focused on much else. "Ah...I don't know."

Mr. Pascal pointed to yesterday's date, November 21, on the blackboard and to the assignment written next to it. "You were supposed to read pages 210-215 last night. Was that not clear?"

"Yes, sir. I—"

Static from the PA system saved Jo from coming up with an excuse, and the principal came on. "Pardon the interruption."

Students looked at each other in surprise at hearing Mr. Peters himself. Usually, the receptionist at the front desk made the announcements, or sometimes Mrs. Flannery, his secretary. Sounds of papers being shuffled filtered over the intercom.

"Maybe school's closing because of the weather," Rosalie whispered.

"It's not snowing that hard," Jo whispered back.

"Maybe the weather forecast has changed," Rosalie replied, careful not to let Mr. Pascal hear. "We can't bring our transistors to school, so how would we know?"

Jo smiled. "Wishful thinking."

Rosalie giggled. "I could use an extra day off."

"Pardon the interruption," the principal said again. "I...I have an announcement to make." This was followed by silence. Jo and Rosalie exchanged glances.

The intercom crackled. "At 1:31 pm this afternoon, President Kennedy was shot in a motorcade in Dallas." The pause that ensued was filled with the collective gasp of the class, and then the principal continued. "The President of the United States is dead."

Another pause. "School is dismissed for the day."

Jo sat back, stunned. President Kennedy was dead. How could that have happened? Who would have done such a thing? And why?

Suddenly, having an extra day off didn't seem to matter.

Chapter Eleven

Summer 1965

Jo looked out at fields of soybeans and wheat rushing past the windows of the bus like a checkerboard of green and yellow squares. Once again, she was headed back to her aunt's farm in Minnesota. She had hoped to go back. She just hadn't ever thought it would be like this. Jo clenched her hands in her lap to keep them from shaking and closed her eyes as she leaned back on the headrest.

She just hadn't ever thought it would be like this.

****

"Coming!" she called as she clamored down the stairs of her parents' home when the doorbell rang. Briefly she wondered if she should grab a jacket, but it was a beautiful early spring day. She couldn't understand why her parents preferred to keep their noses buried in South American history at the library on such a gorgeous day. The sun was shining, the sky was a blue not often seen in the city, and she and Rosalie were headed over to Prospect Park to sit by the water and enjoy the smells of fresh green grass and April flowers. Besides, she'd just bought a Rolling Stones T-shirt she didn't want to cover up.

"Just a sec!" she yelled as the doorbell rang again. *Geez.* Rosalie was early. Grabbing her purse, she slung it over her shoulder and opened the door. "Okay! I'm ready. What's…?" She stopped, staring at the two police officers on the stoop.

"Are you looking for someone?"

One of the officers glanced down at his small, black notepad. "Are you Joleen Thompson?"

"Yes." She frowned. "But I didn't do anything."

The other cop, who looked about the same age as her dad, attempted a tight smile that failed. "I'm afraid there's been an accident. May we come in?"

"An accident? What kind of—"

"It would be better if we could explain inside," the first one said.

"Ah…sure. Come in." Jo opened the door wider and stepped aside. "The living room is over there."

"Thanks. Maybe you should have a seat."

The room suddenly darkened as though a cloud had crossed over the sunlight streaming in the window as a feeling of dread seeped through Jo. "Has something happened to my parents?"

"There's been a car accident over on Fulton, close to Flatbush. A big rig skidded on an oil slick and smashed against two cars." The younger officer looked to the older one and then at her. "Your parents were driving in one of those cars."

Jo inhaled sharply. Her parents had just purchased a secondhand car a few weeks ago since they weren't planning another archeological expedition until sometime next year. They'd thought it a great idea to "tour the country" this summer as part of Jo's education and were planning to stop in Minnesota to visit Aunt Viv.

"So they're in the hospital? How badly are they hurt?"

The officers exchanged a look and then the older one answered. "I'm afraid they're gone. There weren't any survivors."

****

She had never, ever, expected her visit to Minnesota to be like this. Jo slowly opened her eyes and wiped her cheek, although she'd shed all the tears in weeks past. The bus's engine hummed as it kept a steady pace, burning up the miles and taking her far away from the city.

Jo felt torn, as though she were two different people. The thirteen-year-old girl who had come back to Brooklyn two years ago had really not had a care in the world, except for missing her horse and having a silly crush on a boy who had only been friendly. Luke hadn't written in over a year, and Wendy's letters had dwindled to only two or three, as well. Jo really had no idea what was going on in their lives.

President Kennedy's assassination had turned the world topsy-turvy. She and her mother had been glued to the television for the next four days, following every bit of news and practically spellbound by the official proceedings. Jo remembered her mother saying how sorry she felt for Caroline and John-John, being left without a father at such a young age. At the time, Jo never thought something like that could happen to her.

The rest of 1963 had dragged on. It wasn't until February of 1964 when Ed Sullivan invited the Beatles to perform on his show that the darkness hovering over the country seemed to lift, at least for teens. Ironically, as Mr. Pascal pointed out, the second British Invasion seemed more welcome than the first. Jo remembered the blank looks on most of the students' faces over that remark, even though they had just studied the American Revolution. Instead, a lot of the girls started speaking with fake British accents—she had been one of them—while the boys decided to let their hair grow into bangs.

How childish it seemed now.

Jo felt the familiar lump in her throat begin to build again, and she swallowed hard. She had spent enough time crying. The past two and a half months had passed in a blur. Rosalie's parents had taken her in and helped plan the funeral arrangements. Jo had little memory of the actual memorial service, something the school counselor told her wasn't unusual. She recalled Aunt Viv wanting to come to the funeral, but she'd slipped on ice from a late winter storm and broken her leg. Vaguely, Jo remembered other news—President Johnson sending soldiers to Vietnam, and something called Bloody Sunday that involved Civil Rights marchers—but all that had sort of floated around in her head. Rosalie's father had taken care of getting things packed and put into storage, not that she had cared much. Every item seemed to hold memories of her parents.

At least, she had a place to go. Aunt Viv insisted she come to Minnesota and live with them, that they were her family now. But what would it be like this time? Wendy hadn't written. Being a cousin who visited during the summer was one thing, but having a second "sister" was another. Maybe Wendy didn't want her there permanently. Jo was pretty sure Mary Anne didn't, since she had never written at all.

But Jo truly had no other place to go. Her maternal grandparents were both gone—one dying from cancer and the other from an aneurysm. Her paternal grandmother was taking care of her grandfather, who had

Alzheimer's. Rosalie had a brother and her parents' apartment was cramped. Even though they had let Jo finish out the school year at their place, the arrangement couldn't go on forever. At fifteen, Jo was too young to live on her own and she would be only a sophomore in high school, so that left Aunt Viv's invitation.

But Jo wondered how welcome she would really be.

****

Looking around the room that once again was hers, Jo felt an odd mixture of familiarity and being estranged. The walls of the room were still yellow, the white furniture still there, the colorful quilt still on the bed. New curtains hung at the window and the corduroy chair had been reupholstered in green.

It wasn't so much the sameness or changes made in the room that made thoughts swirl in Jo's head. It was the changes made in her life while the farmhouse remained solidly the same.

She didn't have to worry about Wendy's reaction. She had been waiting at the bus station with Aunt Viv and had hugged Jo so hard she had nearly squeezed all the breath out of her.

Jo glanced at her cousin, lying across the bed on her stomach, head propped up on her elbow. Her hair was longer and she'd grown a couple of inches, but she still giggled a lot and she'd chattered nonstop on the short ride back to the farm.

Taking a seat in the chair, Jo thought about when was the last time she had giggled, or even laughed? Probably the morning before the police officers had arrived at her home. The day she'd been so eager to show off her new Stones shirt, the one she'd chosen over others because she liked the background of the group in a dense forest with sunlight bursting behind them. It was the same picture that was on the back cover of their latest album, and her barely-out-of-college art teacher said it represented hope. Light shining through darkness, especially after last year's race riots and the present talk of sending soldiers to Vietnam.

And how sad that one of the greatest hits on that album was *The Last Time*. Even though the lyrics weren't all that fitting, the title definitely was. Jo was pretty sure that horrible day in April was the last time she had laughed.

"Are you all right?" Wendy asked.

Jo shook her head to clear it and then forced a smile. The school counselor had told her at first she'd feel sad a lot of the time, but eventually, things would cause her to smile again. Minnesota would be a fresh start, the counselor had said. And maybe it was. The heavy weight that Jo felt on her shoulders all the time had lightened a little with each mile the bus had driven. "I'm okay. Where's Mary Anne?"

Wendy rolled her eyes. "Who knows? She spends most of her time in town hanging out with kids I don't know very well."

"She isn't dating Tim anymore?"

"They broke up several months ago. He's dating someone else."

"So Mary Anne is hanging out in town now?"

"She isn't supposed to, but she has her driver's license, and when Mom broke her leg, Mary Anne offered to run all the errands. That was great, but with the big casino opening last year over in the next county, we've had lots of strangers in Middletown. The motel is usually full these days. Plus, we had some new folks move into town last month, just before school let out."

"Are they bad people?"

Wendy shrugged. "Probably not. They're from the Twin Cities, and the dads all work at the manufacturing plant down the road. They've rented three houses in town, but they kinda stick to themselves. No one has seen them in church or anything."

"And they have kids our age?"

"There are a bunch of kids, but most of them are in grade school and middle school. The ones in high school are named Ken and Frank, I think, and the girl's Ruby. They'll all be juniors."

"Well, if Mary Anne likes them, they may be okay."

Wendy snorted. "Mary Anne likes them because they're from the cities. She thinks that makes them sophisticated or something. If you ask me, Ruby wears way too much makeup and her dresses are too tight. The guys drive loud cars with no mufflers and look like greasers."

Jo frowned. "Greasers?"

"Yeah, you know…guys who still wear their hair slicked back with oil, as opposed to the Mods who wear their hair like the Beatles. Didn't you use the term in New York?"

"I guess not," Jo answered, "but that reminds me of that other guy your mom didn't like. Bob somebody. Is he still around?"

"Bob Colby. Yeah. He failed some courses, so he's going to be a senior again. He still lives with that uncle who's almost a hermit. Funny thing is…Bob's a lot like these new kids—hair slicked back and a loud car—but he doesn't like them. I think it's because he's really stuck on Mary Anne."

Jo raised an eyebrow. "Your mom lets her see him?"

Wendy shook her head. "No, but I think Mary Anne sneaks out sometimes."

"She's going to get herself into trouble."

"Yeah, I know. I haven't been able to catch her, but some mornings she's really tired. When she was dating Tim, things seemed to be okay. Then they broke up and she started talking to Bob again. Since Mom only got the cast off her leg a couple of weeks ago, it's been real easy for Mary Anne to get out." A look of concern crossed Wendy's face. "Maybe, with you here, we can keep an eye on her."

Jo nodded. "We can try, I guess. Tell me what else has been happening."

Wendy sat up, criss-crossing her legs on the bed and looking glad to change the subject. "We've started a riding club! We call ourselves the Hill Riders"

"Who is *we*?"

"The kids I hang around with. You remember the two parochial schools? They end in the eighth grade, and there's a country school a few miles on the other side of town that only goes to eighth grade too, so last year my class grew by almost twenty kids. Several of them had horses, and Tommy and Tim decided to get into riding with us. It was Tim's idea to form the club. We go on group rides on Saturdays. Mom still has Flame, so you'll have a horse to ride too."

Flame. Jo hadn't thought much about horses in the past two months, and she didn't know if her aunt had sold the mare since she didn't ride much, but Jo perked up a little at the thought of the horse still here. "I'd like to go see her."

"You'll have to wait until tomorrow," Wendy

replied. "The horses are in the lower pasture right now because the grazing is good there. We'll go get them in the morning."

"It'll be good to ride again."

"We're even thinking of entering the horse show at the county fair in September. There's another riders' group from Johannsville who call themselves the Raiders, and they'll be there too. Just about everyone rides Western, but Tim wants to do an English jumping exhibition if the county will let us. Some of the kids like the idea of riding English style—and Tim says it will really show up the other club."

Jo remembered how insistent Tim had been about English saddles when the twins got back from England. "How many people are in the Hill Riders?"

"Twelve, but usually only about seven or eight of us ride at a time, depending on what everyone has to do."

Jo hesitated and then asked, "Does Luke ride?"

"Yeah, when he can. He's still helping Mom around here and, of course, he works on his dad's farm too."

So she would probably run into him soon.

"Varsity sports kept him pretty busy last year." Wendy giggled. "And then Amy moved here from Mankato."

"Amy?"

"Amy Patterson. Her folks bought the corner drug store this spring and started selling a bunch of different flavors of ice cream along with the sodas. She's really cute and popular. I'm pretty sure she'll make cheerleader this fall. And, she has an Arabian horse. He's beautiful! Just wait until you see him!"

Jo had a sinking feeling in her stomach. Luke's horse, Silver Chief, was an Arabian too. "So…she and

Luke have the same breed of horse. Does he like that?"

"I guess." Wendy giggled again. "At least, he likes Amy. He's been dating her since she moved here."

Chapter Twelve

As Wendy left to get ready for supper, Jo tried to contemplate all the changes that had taken place in Middletown over the past two years, to say nothing of the shock at learning Luke was dating someone. Not that she should be shocked. He would be a senior next year and guys his age dated. Still. The last she'd heard from Luke was a Christmas card where he'd scribbled a message asking whether she'd be visiting this summer. Aunt Viv and Wendy had asked the same thing, so she shouldn't have gotten all excited about such a casual question. Even her mother had cautioned her not to read anything into short letters that came once every two or three months in the beginning and had lessened the past year.

Luke hadn't ever said he'd missed her. Obviously, he hadn't since he was dating that Amy person. The one who'd probably be a cheerleader in the fall.

Life goes on, her mother had always said. Of course, her mother hadn't known... Jo bit her lip as tears threatened to well up again. The school counselor had told her when the sadness hit to try and think of something happy. Only it was hard. Jo knew coming to Minnesota was kind of an escape, but she hadn't realized just how much she wanted to see Luke again. Now, whatever silly little hope she'd been holding onto was gone. He was dating someone else. Jo closed her eyes. If she could accept what happened to her parents, she could accept this. She could.

Slowly, from the back of her mind came the familiar lyrics of "*Que Sera Sera.*" Whatever will be, will be.

It was one of her mother's favorite songs.

****

Jo received her second shock of the day when she reached the kitchen an hour later. She hardly recognized the girl standing at the counter She must be Mary Anne, but her eyes were ringed in heavy liner, with points extending outward at the far corners. She'd cut her dark hair in an asymmetrical style with one side super short and the other angled down at a slope to her chin, but it was her clothes that made Jo stifle a gasp.

Mary Anne wore tight tan stretch pants with knee high boots and a Grateful Dead T-shirt under a black leather jacket. Jo frowned, remembering that a disc jockey in New York had mentioned them. They were some weird group that had just formed in San Francisco and experimented with a drug called LSD. According to Rosalie's dad, who was a pharmacist, it was dangerous but not illegal. Did Mary Anne know about that? And where had she gotten the T-shirt anyway?

Mary Anne smiled slowly, as though enjoying the shock Jo pretty much felt was on her face, and then looked Jo up and down.

"I see your fashion sense hasn't changed."

In spite of herself, Jo felt her face warm as she looked down at her plain Oxford shirt tucked into a plaid skirt. The outfit had met her school dress code and she hadn't had any interest in shopping this spring. "I guess not."

"Well, it probably doesn't matter in this hokey

town." Mary Anne picked up her soda pop bottle and moved toward the dining room. "I can't wait to move to Minneapolis where the action is."

"But you have to finish school first." Jo followed her cousin.

"Maybe."

Jo nearly tripped over her own feet as she abruptly stopped. Mary Anne couldn't mean she was thinking of dropping out, could she? Jo had seen too many kids who had dropped out of high school hanging around on Brooklyn's street corners. Hoodlums, Rosalie's mother had called them, and even Jo's parents said those kids were headed for a life of crime. How did Mary Anne think she could support herself in the cities?

What in the world had gotten into her cousin? One thing was for sure. She and Wendy would have to keep an eye on Mary Anne.

****

After the major news she'd received on her first day back, it was a relief to walk with Wendy the next morning to the lower pasture and experience something familiar…the horses. Wendy's bay, Jupiter, and Aunt Viv's sorrel, Flame, were at the far end. Both of them raised their heads as Wendy and Jo approached the fence.

Even from this distance, Jo could see Flame flick her ears forward as she scented the air. To Jo's delight, the mare started trotting toward them.

"She remembers you!" Wendy said.

"Do you really think so? It's been two years."

"Horses are smart," Wendy replied. "You were always gentle with her."

"Yeah, and I always brought her a treat to eat," Jo answered, pulling some plastic-wrapped apple slices out of her jeans pocket. She unwrapped them and put them on the fence post. "Maybe this is what she remembers."

"I think she saw that," Wendy said as the mare cantered toward them with Jupiter following at a trot.

"You'd better have something in your pocket for Jupiter."

"Oh, I do." Wendy took out slices of apple too and held them up. Jupiter broke into a gallop at the sight and Flame, not to be outdone, picked up her pace as well. Both horses skidded to a stop inches from the fence.

To Jo's surprise, Flame lifted her head over the boards to nuzzle Jo instead of guzzling the apples. The horse's velvety muzzle grazed her cheek and then nudged gently at her shoulder. Tears—of happiness this time—welled in Jo's eyes as she threw her arms around the mare's neck. "It's so good to see you, girl. I've missed you so, so much!" As if in understanding, Flame nickered softly and then pawed the ground with one hoof.

"Oh, okay!" Jo laughed at the horse's impatience and wiped tears away at the same time. "Enough hugging. You want your treat."

In response, Flame tossed her head and snorted.

Jo fed her the apple slices one at a time to prolong the moment. She knew she'd missed the mare, but until right now she hadn't known how much. Flame had even made her laugh.

"We just brought halter leads," Wendy said, "but I'll bet the horses will head straight for the barn if you want to ride back."

"Yes, let's!" Jo watched as Wendy hooked her lead to Jupiter's halter and climbed the fence to perch on the top rail, tugging at the gelding to come closer. Jo scampered up too. As if sensing her intent, Flame sidled over to allow her to climb on. With no saddle, she could feel the mare's every muscle move beneath her silky coat. The feeling was strange, and yet she felt so much a part of the horse. "I've never ridden bareback before."

"Use your thighs and grab the mane if you have to," Wendy answered, "but I doubt they'll run since it's uphill."

The ride was short, less than a half mile, but Jo could feel her legs wobble when she slid down at the barn. "I've really got to get back into shape."

"You will." Wendy led Jupiter inside and put him in his stall. "I'm going up to the house to get a snack since I skipped breakfast."

"I think I'll stay here with Flame for a little bit and brush her out."

"Okay. After lunch we can saddle them and go for a real ride."

"Sounds good." Jo attached the end of the mare's lead to an iron ring in the wall and walked over to the tack room to get the currycomb and brush from the shelf where the grooming supplies were. At least everything here was still the same. Bridles hung on pegs, and saddles sat on wooden sawhorses, with blankets spread across the seats to air. The smell of leather mixed with hay was comforting. Jo crooned softly to the horse as she brushed and combed. Flame's head drooped, her eyes half-closed in contentment as she blew through her nose. Jo gave the shiny coat a final pat and put Flame in her stall. "It feels so good to be back."

"It's good to have you back."

Jo started, nearly dropping the comb and brush. She took a deep breath and turned to face Luke.

He leaned against the door frame, one leg bent with his boot against the wall, thumbs hooked in the pockets of his jeans, watching her. Luke was taller than she remembered, and more muscular too, but then, it had been two years. He wore his black hair longer now, the edges brushing the collar of his chambray shirt. Once again, she felt as tongue-tied as she had the first time she'd met him.

He didn't seem to notice her discomfort. Instead, he came inside, nodding toward Flame, who'd stuck her head over the half-door. 'I swear, the first month you were gone, she got depressed."

"I'm depressed too— I mean, I was depressed. When I first left."

Luke gave her an apprising look. "Hey. We all heard what happened. It's okay to be down."

"Thanks." Jo managed a small smile. "The counselor said I was supposed to think of happy things when I got…down."

"Probably good advice. You were happy here before. You will be again."

Jo nodded, not trusting her voice. Luke had been a big reason for her happiness two years ago. Now he was dating someone else. Did he even remember their kiss? Probably not. It had only been a sweet kiss, she realized now, but it had lingered huge in her mind for months. She turned away. "I think I'd better go. Wendy was making snacks for us."

"Let me take those." Luke held out his hand for the brush and comb.

Jo felt her face warm. Why did her mind suddenly stop working around Luke? Geez. She'd just about walked to the house with grooming equipment.

"Okay." Jo held them out, and that strange tingle she hadn't felt in two years coursed up her arm as his fingers closed over hers briefly. She dropped her hand. "I gotta go."

"Okay," Luke replied, his voice sounding funny. "See you soon."

"Soon." Jo forced herself to walk away and not run. *Soon.* She was going to have to get used to seeing Luke again, and she was going to have to get over this stupid crush she had on him.

A crush she thought she'd gotten over a year ago.

****

"Isn't Mary Anne going to join us for breakfast?" Jo asked the next morning as Aunt Viv dished out scrambled eggs and crisp slices of bacon.

"Not her," Wendy said, buttering toast. "She can't get up before noon."

"Noon?"

"That's an exaggeration," Aunt Viv said with a tired smile.

"Not by much," Wendy answered and set down the plate of toast.

"Well, it's summer, and she does listen to the radio until late at night."

Wendy exchanged a glance with Jo and Jo wondered if having the radio on was a distraction so Mary Anne could sneak out at night. She'd have to ask Wendy later.

They had just finished washing the dishes when Jo heard horses' hooves pounding up the yard road. She gave Wendy a questioning look.

"The riding club is here," Wendy said. "It's Saturday."

The riding club. Was Luke with them? He'd said,

See you soon. Jo wasn't quite ready to have it be this soon though. Her feelings were still all swirling around in her head like flavors on a banana split. And…she really had to prepare herself to see him with his girlfriend. She needed more time.

"Ah…why don't you ride without me today? I'm feeling kind of tired from the long trip and everything."

"Phooey. You've had plenty of time to rest," Wendy replied. "Besides, I told Tim and Tommy you were back and they want to see you." She tossed the towel on the kitchen counter. "Come on. You can sleep later."

"Go ahead," Aunt Viv said. "Have some fun. It'll do you a world of good."

Since she couldn't tell her aunt the real reason she didn't want to go riding, Jo reluctantly followed Wendy out the door. She scanned the yard quickly, but no grey Arabian was among the horses, which meant Luke hadn't come. Jo let out a small sigh of relief, only to feel nervous again as a girl with long golden hair dismounted gracefully from a prancing, coal-black horse and came forward with a big smile.

"Hi, I'm Amy. You must be Jo. Welcome back. I've heard so much about you."

From whom? Jo wanted to ask, but didn't. She tried not to stare. Wendy had said Amy was pretty, but this girl looked like a movie star, tall and slim and gorgeous.

"Hey! Don't I get a hug?" Tim asked, saving Jo from having to reply to Amy.

"Me, too," Tommy said, following on Tim's heels. "It's really good to see you!"

Jo was spared answering them too as she was smothered by the twins trying to both hug her at the same time and getting into a tussling match as they did. Wendy punched both of them on their shoulders. "Let her breathe, for Pete's sake!"

They laughed as they stepped back and, as Jo was straightening her shirt, she noticed two girls still mounted who weren't smiling. Amy must have seen her look because she turned to the girls. "Carla. Susan. Aren't you going to get down and come say hi?"

Tommy went to help one of them—Susan, Jo thought it was—while the other dismounted by herself and went straight to Tim and put her arm around his waist. She gave Jo a look any girl out of elementary school would know was a warning to stay away. Jo tried not to smile. The girl—Carla?—didn't have to worry about that. Nor did Susan, although her look was less hostile.

"How do you like our new horses?" Tommy asked.

Jo was only too happy to turn her attention to their animals. They were a pair of matched chestnuts with white blazes, which didn't surprise Jo. Since the twins liked to be identical so they could pull practical jokes, it made sense their horses would look the same. And it was hardly surprising that the horses looked like Thoroughbreds and were under English saddle. She knew the twins had spent time in England, which accounted for the saddles. "They're beautiful. Where did you get them?"

"Dad bought them in Kentucky off a racehorse breeder," Tommy answered.

"We're trying to get our girlfriends and Amy to switch over to English gear," Tim said, "so we can ride in more shows."

"English style is really wonderful to watch," Amy said with a tactful smile, "but we'd be risking our horses without proper training in jumping techniques."

A sensation as heavy as a rock settled in Jo's stomach. Luke had said almost those same words the summer she was here. And she had to admit he—and Amy—were right. Except for Jupiter, the other horses probably weren't used to jumping.

"Since you're from New York, you've probably ridden English," Amy said to Jo. "Which style do you prefer?"

"Uh…I guess either one." Geez. She sounded stupid. "I mean…it kind of depends on what the horse is used to."

"You are so right!" Amy flashed her big smile at Jo again. "Fury wouldn't like to switch styles."

Fury? Jo's mind flitted to the old TV series she'd watched as a child. That Fury had a white star on its forehead, but the name seemed to fit, given the beauty of this Fury. "I've seen Arabians at the Madison Square Garden Horse Show both ways."

"You've been to that horse show? It's the best in the country!" Amy looked delighted. "Maybe you could help me train Fury for the county fair?"

"That'd be fun!" Wendy said before Jo could answer. "We can practice Western Pleasure and…" She turned to Tim and Tommy, "…whoever gets the least points at the fair has to clean out all the stables for the riding club!"

"You're on," the twins said in unison.

"Good," Wendy replied. "Now let's ride!"

"Yes, let's!" Amy said and linked her arm to Jo's. "I'm so glad you decided to come back to Minnesota. We're going to have so much fun, don't you think?"

Jo didn't want to think, especially about being

friends with Amy and having to watch her and Luke together.

And why did Amy have to be so friendly and nice?

Chapter Thirteen

Jo crossed the small clearing toward the pines that hid the stone hut from view unless someone knew it was there. She had surprised herself by remembering the way along the winding path through the trees after two years. The first time Wendy had led her here, she'd thought the way confusing since there were several trails that led off from the main one. She'd thought about waiting for Wendy to join her, but her cousin and Aunt Viv had gone into town after supper to visit an ailing, retired teacher whom Wendy had been with in first grade. Mary Anne had disappeared into her room, which left Jo with nothing to do.

Besides, she really wanted to visit the cabin by herself.

Jo rounded the trees and stopped. From the outside, it looked the same. A stack of firewood was piled along one side. The wood around the window panes had weathered, but the door was firmly set on its hinges, instead of hanging loose like the first time she saw it. Was it locked? She hadn't thought of that.

To her relief the door opened easily. Jo peered cautiously inside and then shook her head as she stepped inside. What was she expecting to find? Wild animals? Like that fake wolf howl that had scared her to pieces and sent her scurrying for cover the first time? She really had been a child back then, thinking the wolf was real and letting Wendy frighten her.

Jo looked around. The inside of the hut was pretty much the same too, although the quilts on the cot had been replaced with fleece blankets. A partly burned log lay in the hearth and the tins on the counter held snacks, indicating the cabin was probably used recently. Did Wendy still come here? Did Luke?

At least it was empty today. Jo wanted to be alone with her thoughts right now.

She remembered the conversation she and Wendy had when they'd come here that first time. Wendy had made it seem Luke liked her as a girlfriend, although her mom wouldn't allow her to date. Jo had believed her and gotten upset. Looking back, all that seemed so silly now.

Now Luke had a real girlfriend.

Jo pulled out a chair and sat, placing her elbows on the table and putting her forehead in her hands. What was she going to do? She knew she'd had a childish crush on Luke, but she really thought she'd gotten over it last year when she started high school and boys had actually started to flirt with her. Their remarks—and sometimes their advances, which she rejected—had made her realize that the few letters Luke had sent were short and about school or the horses and nothing personal.

Since her parents were killed, Jo hadn't thought much about anything. In those first weeks, her mind had been numb. Moving was required, breathing was required. Eating—and eventually exhausted sleep—were required. She had pretty much lived in zombie-land, with Rosalie attending classes with her, classes she had no recollection of. Only in May, when she passed her tests, did she realize the teachers had cut her a lot of slack. The Matteos had taken care of everything else.

Even when Aunt Viv insisted she come live with them, her brain had only registered that the farm would be a safe haven. She desperately wanted—needed—to get away from Brooklyn and all that it reminded her of. A fresh start would be good, the school counselor had said.

And it had taken only a brief conversation with Luke to make all her old memories and dead feelings come alive. Memories and feelings that were useless now.

Luke had a girlfriend.

The tears Jo had been holding back since she'd found out suddenly flowed down her cheeks like torrents of rain from a cloudburst. Her sobs grew louder, echoing off the stone walls, but she didn't care. No one was here. No one would know. She was, for the first time since her parents' death, alone. Alone. She thought she heard a wolf howl, only to realize the sound was coming from her own throat.

And it felt good.

****

Jo opened her eyes to twilight beginning to settle in the cabin and sat up quickly. She must have fallen asleep after she'd drained herself of tears. She remembered putting her head down on her arms…

She looked at her watch and gave a relieved sigh. It was only 7:30 p.m. Aunt Viv and Wendy would probably still be in town since Wendy had dropped hints all afternoon about stopping for ice cream before they came home. Still, Jo had to get back.

She re-entered the woods feeling a lot better than when she'd arrived. Her face probably looked all blotchy and her eyes swollen and red, but the cry had done her some good. She even felt like she might be able to face

Luke again...she'd think about that tomorrow, though. Maybe she'd even put on a sunny face in the morning.

Jo paused as she came to the fork in the trail that led down to the river. With no wind rustling the tree leaves, she could hear the water flowing over rocks. Maybe if she spent a few minutes on the riverbank, it would give the swelling of her face time to go down and no one would know she'd been crying.

This trail was narrower and with more twists, but the sound of the water became louder as she made her way through the fern-like vegetation and soft moss. She kept her face down, watching for tree roots or sharp rocks. She didn't need to be twisting an ankle. Jo finally broke through the trees onto the grassy bank and stood watching the water sweep swiftly past.

The bank on the other side was far steeper, forming a long ridge maybe ten feet high. Most of the hill was covered in dense underbrush with granite boulders protruding here and there. Jo caught a flash of something white in the bushes and felt a moment of panic, remembering the young couple who'd tried to elope, only the girl had drowned and was said to haunt the old bridge farther upstream. She chided herself for being so gullible and then gasped in shock as Luke emerged, apparently from nowhere, carrying a fishing pole.

He looked up in surprise. "Hi! What are you doing down here?"

She stared at him, frozen in place.

"Jo?"

She finally found her voice, although it sounded raspy. "I...went to the cabin to think and...decided...I'd stop by the river."

He frowned and lowered his fishing pole. "Have you

been crying?"

Jo's hands flew to her face. Although the river wasn't wide at this spot, her face must really look awful if Luke could see the blotchiness from across the water and in the fading light. "No. I'd better go."

"Wait up. I'll cross over at the bridge and walk you home."

"No! I mean, I'd better get back right now!" She turned and ran, ignoring his shout to wait.

Maybe she could face him tomorrow, when she had her happy face on, but not tonight. Not tonight. She had to get away.

****

Jo stopped running when her side developed a stitch in her side. She leaned over, hands on knees, taking in big gulps of air. Why had she panicked anyhow? She hadn't expected to see Luke, but she'd bolted like a horse out of a pasture gate for no real reason.

She straightened, noticing several tears on her sleeves where raspberry bush thorns had caught her as she raced through the trees. Her cheek stung as well, and she put a hand to her face, finding a trickle of blood. Jo remembered pushing low-hanging branches aside in her mad rush to get away.

To get away from what? Luke? He'd stood on the other bank, looking puzzled. Maybe she was running from herself...or her feelings for him. Feelings she shouldn't have. Feelings she did have. Dear God, she was so confused.

As her heart rate returned to normal, Jo looked around and a cold feeling of dread swept over her skin. She could see no clear path or trail, only lots of trees casting long shadows through the darkening woods. She had no idea where she was.

And then Jo heard a faint rustling from the way she had come—at least she thought she'd come from that direction. The sound grew louder, as though something foraged for food in the undergrowth. Her breath hitched and she reminded herself there were no real wolves in the area…and then she remembered Luke saying the river attracted wildlife at night. How far was she from the river? She couldn't hear any water, but she heard the rustling again. This time, definitely closer. Was an animal stalking her? Jo fought the panicky feeling rising in her again. She shouldn't run. That only would make whatever was out there chase her. Maybe if she walked quietly, she wouldn't alert whatever it was.

Turning, she promptly tripped over a fallen tree trunk and fell forward with a small cry. Scrambling to stand, she slipped on the slick moss under the dislodged trunk and skidded onto her stomach. More rustling. The animal was really close now…

"Jo? Jo? Where are you?"

Jo went weak with relief at the sound of Luke's voice, forgetting she hadn't wanted to see him. "Over here!"

He burst through a tall fern patch as she was scurrying to regain her footing. In two strides, he was beside her, one arm around her middle, lifting her to her feet. Then both hands encircled her waist, steadying her while she regained her balance.

"Are you okay? Why did you run?"

"I…I don't know."

"You don't know if you're okay or you don't know why you ran?"

All Jo knew right now was her tummy was fluttering

with restless butterflies. She drew a shaky breath. "I…I'm okay."

"Are you sure?" Luke asked as he slowly dropped his hands.

"Yeah." To prove her point, Jo shifted her weight from one foot to the other and managed to stay standing although her knees felt like gelatin. "I just feel stupid."

Luke looked like he was about to say something but thought better of it. "Well, then, we'd better get you home."

"I'm lost. Do you know where we are?"

Luke smiled, the look of worry leaving his face. "You may think you're lost, but your instincts took you home." He pointed to his left. "Mrs. Wade's farm is just over there. Come on. You'll see the house in just a few more minutes."

Sure enough. They'd walked less than five minutes when Jo glimpsed the white farmhouse through the trees. "Now I really feel stupid."

"Don't," Luke said. "The woods can be confusing. It's easy to get lost."

"How did you find me?"

"You left a pretty good trail with all the broken branches and trampled grass." He grinned. "Remember, I am part Ojibwa."

Jo smiled back. "And you were born with tracking skills?"

"Nah. But my dad did send me off to Indian cultural camps Up North for a couple of summers. One of the programs was tracking moose, bear, and wolves."

"That sounds scary. What if one of them had attacked you?"

"I don't think twelve- and thirteen-year-old boys

think about danger. We thought it'd be cool if we saw any of them."

Jo suppressed a shudder. "I'm just glad I didn't see anything like that here."

"These woods are pretty safe, at least from animals."

"What do you mean?"

Luke shrugged. "Some of the kids like to go by the old bridge on weekends and party. A few of them get drunk."

"But they're underage."

"Well, they seem to know where to get booze. And it's not just kids from Middletown. Last year a couple of girls made it to the highway with their clothes torn. They said some guys from Giddesberg, down the road, had attacked them. A farmer picked them up and took them home."

"Were the boys found?"

Luke shook his head. "The girls only had first names, and those were probably fake ones. Anyway," he said as they broke through the trees and entered the farmyard, "it's best not to go into the woods at night."

"I'll remember that. Thanks for finding me tonight."

"My dad would be pretty disappointed if I hadn't been able to." He looked toward the house. "Do you want me to come in with you and explain?"

Jo shook her head quickly. The last thing she needed was for her aunt to think she'd been out in the woods chasing Luke, even if he had a different explanation for it. "I'll just tell them I lost track of time."

"Okay then." Luke's gaze lingered on her face for a moment and his hand came forward before he checked himself and turned the movement into a wave. "See you."

"See you," Jo answered as she watched him walk away. Then she turned and made her way up to the house.

****

Jo hobbled into the parlor the next afternoon where Tim and Tommy, along with their girlfriends and Amy, were clustered around the card table looking at guidelines for various events at the county fair horse show. She tried not to wince, but her ribs hurt at every step. She'd landed harder than she'd thought when she tripped over that log.

"Oh, my goodness! What on earth happened to you?" Amy asked in concern. "You can hardly walk."

"And you've got scratches on your face and hands," Tommy said.

Tim laughed. "You look like you got into a fight."

"No fight," Jo answered. "I just fell."

"Into a patch of thistles or something?"

Jo shook her head, wishing they'd stop asking questions. Wendy and Aunt Viv had asked enough of those last night. They'd been getting ready to go searching for her—even Mary Anne had been at the door—when Jo had walked in with her shirt torn and grass-stained along with the scratches on her skin. Aunt Viv thought she'd been attacked. Jo had told them she'd gone to the river and then gotten scared when she saw someone and had run home. It wasn't so far from the truth, but Jo couldn't bring herself to say she'd been running from Luke. Wendy, for sure, would think she was crazy. Her aunt had launched into a lecture about not going into the woods alone and then questions about why she'd gone to the river in the first place. It wasn't until Mary Anne suggested that maybe Jo wanted to jump in and her aunt had asked if that were true that Jo realized they thought she might actually harm herself. The counselor had asked the same kind of questions just before school was out. Jo had started crying then, and her aunt had bustled her off to bed, looking very worried. She'd looked relieved when Jo came to breakfast with a bright smile on her face. And then the look had turned to concern again when Jo nearly fainted from pain.

"I went for a walk in the woods and got lost, and then panicked." Jo hoped that would end the conversation.

Instead, Tim hooted. "Maybe we need to get you a compass."

"Oh, leave her alone," Wendy snapped back. "The doctor said she's bruised a rib, maybe even cracked it."

"Well, geez," Tim said, the smile leaving his face. "Why didn't you say so? Here. Do you want my chair?"

"Thank you," Jo said, causing Carla to frown at her.

"Can I get you a soda pop or something?" Tommy asked and then headed to the kitchen without waiting for a reply. "I'll be right back."

"Maybe you should go lie down in your room instead," Susan said.

Amy looked at her and then at Carla. "Jo should be a part of the plans for the show. If she wants to lie down, she can use the sofa." Amy smiled at her. "I cracked a rib once, skiing Up North, and it felt better when I sat up."

So Amy had been Up North. Luke had grown up along Lake Superior, Up North. Did he ski too? What else did they have in common? Jo bit her lip, knowing her thoughts were unkind. Why did Amy have to be the nice one?

Tommy brought in the can of pop and set in on the

table. "All I could find was root beer."

"That's fine, thanks."

"Do you want ice?" Tim asked.

"No," Jo said quickly when both Carla and Susan glared at the twins. Then she winced as she shifted in her chair to reach for the soda.

"Let me." Amy moved the can toward her and then got up to get a throw pillow from the sofa. "This might help," she said as she placed it behind Jo. "I remember how much it hurt."

"Thanks," Jo replied, ashamed of herself for being jealous of Amy. She was kind and helpful and nice to everyone. No wonder Luke liked her.

Not that it made Jo feel any better. She winced again, but not from physical pain.

Somehow she was going to have to put Luke out of her mind.

Chapter Fourteen

Since the doctor had told her to rest—or at least not be very active—Jo had taken to watching TV. She really liked watching *The Avengers* since Mr. Steed always ended up needing the help of a female assistant agent. The women were pretty, but they were also smart, especially Emma Peel.

Too bad they couldn't fix things in real life, because the daily news wasn't that good. Five hundred blacks recently had been arrested in Jackson, Mississippi, for marching on the capitol and demanding fair voting laws. Half of them had been teenagers and were taken away in garbage trucks to the county fairgrounds and "jailed" in livestock pens. Jo thought about the local county fairgrounds. She remembered walking through the various barns two years ago. They'd been filled with 4-H cattle, pigs and sheep. The straw on the floor had been fresh and the pens hadn't smelled, but she couldn't imagine putting people in there as prisoners.

And then there was the war, although officially it wasn't called that. Still, more and more boys were being drafted into the Army right out of high school. Some were defiant, burning their draft cards or going to Canada. Protests were being held everywhere, from Hyde Park in London to New York's Madison Square Garden and even at the Pentagon.

Jo had cried over the song "There But for Fortune"

since her parents' death, but now she was thinking of the lyrics in a different light. It made her sad to think that the Garden should be filled with so many angry people. One of the best times in her life had been the horse show there. Tim and Tommy's dad had been in Washington when the Pentagon protest happened, and he'd come home a few days ago angry too. Why?

"Why?" Aunt Viv repeated when Jo asked her one night at supper. "A lot of folks don't want us fighting a war halfway around the world, especially when our boys are in actual combat and could get killed."

Jo sucked in a breath. Luke would be a senior this year. If he didn't get into a college after graduation, he would probably be drafted too. She didn't want to think about that. "Maybe the war won't last long."

Aunt Viv shook her head. "These things have a way of dragging on and on. I remember Korea. That lasted three years. And the World Wars even longer."

"But Uncle Martin says if we don't help, South Vietnam will be taken over by Communists," Wendy said as she finished her bowl of ice cream.

"That's true too," her mother said.

"Do you think Tim and Tommy will go fight?"

Mary Anne looked up quickly from her plate. "Why would they?"

"Jeepers Jenny," Wendy said in exasperation. "Don't you ever watch anything on TV besides *The Dating Game* and *Hullabaloo*? Vietnam is all over the news!"

Mary Anne rolled her eyes. "The news is depressing."

"It is," Jo agreed, "but that doesn't mean it's going to go away."

"Sadly, you're right," Aunt Viv said before Mary Anne could retort, "but to answer the question, I'm sure the twins will be going to college. Even if the war isn't over by the time they graduate, Martin is an Army colonel. He can get them into Officer Candidate School and probably assigned somewhere safe."

Jo bit her lip. Would Luke be so lucky?

****

Ten days later the bruised rib was still sore, but at least Jo could move without scrunching her face into a grim mask with each step. After her aunt had broken her leg, she'd strung a hammock between two trees alongside the house in order to keep her leg elevated. Jo found that lying in it was more comfortable than being in her bed. She had less pressure on her back, and the gentle sway was almost like a cradle, lulling her to sleep.

Since the June evenings were warm, she'd taken to spending the nights outside, although she waited until everyone had gone to bed to go back downstairs. Aunt Viv would just worry more if she thought Jo couldn't sleep. Shortly after her trip to the river—and after her remark about the TV news being bad—Jo had found a book from the local library dealing with depression tucked away in her aunt's magazine rack. She was pretty sure Aunt Viv didn't want her to see it.

While she did feel depressed sometimes, Jo wished she could convince everyone she hadn't meant anything by going down to the river. She'd only wanted to listen to the water and watch it stream by. She'd worry her aunt more if she told her the real reason she'd run was because she saw Luke. It did seem pretty silly now.

Jo didn't think Luke had told Amy about what happened either. Although the riding group had been over only twice since the incident—once to ride on Saturday and Jo couldn't go—Amy had been friendly both times and hadn't mentioned anything.

Luke had been over only once. It had been a wet spring and farmers were late in getting their crops planted. He'd come over to replace a garage door for Aunt Viv and seemed surprised, when he came into the kitchen for cookies and lemonade, to learn Jo had hurt her ribs. Wendy had chattered on about how Jo had seen some hoodlums by the river and run away scared and then fallen. Luke had given Jo a quizzical look, but made no comment on her version of events. He only said he hoped she'd be feeling better soon.

It wasn't until after he left that Jo realized she hadn't felt any pain until the next morning. Did Luke think she was making this up? When he'd helped her stand and walked her home, she'd only been thinking about him.

Jo shook her head and sighed. She had to stop thinking about Luke. No wonder she couldn't sleep.

She looked up at the night sky, illuminated by an almost full moon. A few stars twinkled through the leafy canopy of tree branches overhead. The wind had quieted from the day and she could hear crickets chirping as well as the sound of some small animal scurrying among the rosebushes nearby. From the woods, she heard an owl hoot and then all was still.

Tire wheels crunching on gravel at the end of the yard road broke the silence. Jo shifted slightly in the hammock and then watched, amazed, as Mary Anne slipped out of the car. It was well past midnight. When had her cousin snuck out? Jo watched as Mary Anne started toward the house. She tripped, caught herself, and then walked unevenly up the road. She fumbled for something in her purse as she approached the side door and then stopped abruptly when she saw Jo in the hammock.

"Are you spying on me?"

"No. I…I just wanted some fresh air."

Mary Anne took a step closer, her eyes narrowing. "I don't believe you. You were waiting for me."

"I didn't even—"

"Well, you better not tell Mom."

Jo swallowed. "You shouldn't be sneaking out."

"It's none of your business what I do."

"I'm just saying—"

"Just shut up. If you tell Mom, I'll say I saw you from my window, waiting for Luke to pick you up."

"Luke? Why—"

"Oh, don't play stupid. I know you still like him." Mary Anne hiccupped. "Maybe I should tell Amy."

"No! Don't! I mean—"

"Then keep quiet about tonight and maybe I won't." Mary Anne smiled and turned toward the house. "But then, maybe I will. It's up to you."

Jo lay staring at the starry sky for a long time after Mary Anne went in, wondering what to do. She didn't want Amy mad at her. Even worse, Jo didn't want Luke mad at her. Yet…Aunt Viv should know.

Dawn was breaking before Jo finally closed her eyes and drifted off to sleep.

****

"Jo? Jo?" Her aunt's voice broke through fuzzy dreams.

Jo opened her eyes to bright sunshine and struggled to sit up in the swaying hammock. "Is it morning already?"

"It's past nine o'clock. When you didn't come down for breakfast I sent Wendy to get you. She said your bed hadn't been slept in. I didn't know what to think."

Jo felt guilt wash over her. She'd been getting back to her bedroom before daylight. Now Aunt Viv's worried face told her what her aunt didn't say. She probably thought Jo had wandered off again, maybe to the river, even.

"I'm okay, honest." She swung her legs over the edge of the hammock and stood. "This is just more comfortable than a bed."

"You've been spending the nights out here?"

"Yes. It's okay, isn't it? I mean, it's safe, right?"

"I suppose so," Aunt Viv answered, "but I never heard you go out." She rubbed her forehead. "My leg still hurts a lot, and the doctor told me to take a painkiller at night, but maybe I need to stop doing that."

So that's how Mary Anne was sneaking out. Jo felt another wave of guilt wash over her. Should she tell her aunt what happened last night? Maybe if her aunt stopped taking the pills, the problem would be fixed. "Have you tried sleeping without the pill?"

"Yes, but I don't do very well. During the day, I can pretty much ignore that pain, but at night it's hard to rest."

"Yes, I know."

Her aunt glanced at the hammock. "I suppose you do, at that." Then she looked back at Jo. "But is that the only reason you come out here? Are you feeling all right…otherwise?"

Jo nodded. "Honest, Aunt Viv, I'm okay. I feel down sometimes, but I'm okay."

Aunt Viv smiled and put an arm around Jo. "Good.

You know, you can always come and talk to me. About anything. I can't take the place of your mother, but I'm here for you. Now let's go in and get you some breakfast."

"That sounds good," Jo replied and followed her aunt into the house. Aunt Viv had said she could talk to her about anything. But could Jo tell her about Mary Anne?

****

The day Jo had been looking forward to finally arrive—Saturday, and she was finally going to be able to ride again. It had been nearly three weeks since her fall, and the doctor had given permission to ride as long as she didn't do anything strenuous.

She'd been relieved too when she hadn't seen Mary Anne sneak out again, but maybe that was because Jo decided she'd continue to use the hammock until Aunt Viv started feeling better. It would be hard for her cousin to get by her.

"Flame's raring to go," Wendy said as they led their saddled horses out of the barn to wait for the rest of the riders.

"I've missed riding her." Jo patted the silken neck. She'd gone out to the barn every day, delivering apple slices, but she hadn't been able to brush the mare down or do much else, since bending hurt. "I wish I could run her."

"Well, not today," Wendy said. "Mom made me promise we'd only walk the horses. No trotting, even."

"That's going to slow down everyone else, though," Jo said as she saw Tim and Tommy and their girlfriends coming up the road.

"They can gallop off if they want to. I'll stay with

you."

"Thanks, but you don't have to. Flame will behave."

"Yeah, but I'm not sure you will," Wendy answered with a grin. "I know you're itching to run, and Mom will ground me for a week if I let you."

Jo shook her head. "Don't worry. I won't get you into trouble."

The twins had just gotten onto the yard when Jo heard more horses on the road. Glancing in that direction, she felt her breath hitch as she saw Amy's black gelding and Luke's grey stallion headed their way.

Jo swallowed hard, unable to look away as Amy tossed her head back and laughed at something Luke said. Jo knew she was going to have to see them together sooner or later. She just wished it hadn't been today when she'd looked forward to having a super-fun day.

"Wow, Luke's actually coming along," Wendy said, oblivious to Jo's staring. "I wonder if all the planting's done."

"Maybe he just wanted to take a day off."

"Or maybe Amy made him take a day off. She's been saying she's not seen him very much the past month."

The past month. Jo had been here just over a month. Could that mean...? She shook her head, telling herself she was being silly again. Luke hadn't come by to visit after that day in the kitchen. "He probably hasn't had time."

"Yeah. You know the old saying about making hay when the sun shines," Wendy said as she swung into the saddle. "It applies for getting the grain into the ground, too."

Jo led Flame toward a stump she could use as a

mounting block and carefully climbed on just as Luke and Amy joined the group. Luke glanced over at Jo. "How are you feeling?"

"A lot better."

"But the doctor says nothing strenuous," Wendy said.

Amy leaned over and put a hand on Luke's arm. "Jo's been a really good sport about helping us plan some of the horse show events we want to present to the county. "Since she hasn't been able to go riding, she's done all the paperwork."

"It was just a couple of letters," Jo mumbled, trying not to notice the gesture. She wasn't sure if she liked Amy championing her or not.

"Are you going to be okay to ride in it?" Luke asked as Silver Chief pranced sideways away from Amy's horse.

Jo could have kissed the animal. "I should be. It's a good two months away."

"You'll have to practice, though," Susan said. "We don't want anyone in the Hill Riders looking bad."

"Yeah, you have to be able to get your horse to change leads in trotting and cantering without the judges noticing," Carla added. "It's not easy. You probably need to start practicing right away."

"It's not that hard either," Luke said and turned to Jo. "It's a matter of timing. I can show you as soon as the doctor says it's okay."

Amy shot him a quick glance and then smiled at Jo. "Luke's right. It isn't all that hard. We can work together."

"Don't forget that I want Jo and Wendy to do the jumping, too," Tim said.

Luke frowned. "Jupiter has been trained to jump. Flame hasn't."

"I can train the horse to jump," Tim answered.

"And Jo will catch on in no time," Tommy added.

"It's not smart to have someone learn to jump on a horse that isn't well-trained itself," Luke said.

Tim's chin jutted forward. "Tommy and I took lessons in England from one of the best horse masters."

"Doesn't make you an expert."

"I'm pretty sure we can handle it," Tommy said.

"It's dangerous. Jo could get really hurt."

Amy glanced at Luke again. "Maybe we should all ask Jo if she wants to learn to jump or not."

"Oh, I do!" Jo replied quickly. "I've always loved watching *National Velvet*. I know we don't have steeplechases, but to be able to jump like Velvet on her horse King would be—"

"That's TV," Susan said with a laugh, "and probably a stunt double riding, too."

"Besides, we're not even sure the county will let us jump," Carla added, "so why waste Tim and Tommy's time?"

Tommy gave her an incredulous look. "Because we want to beat the Raiders."

"Yeah! And the best way to do that is to show them up," Tim said. "If most of the Hill Riders can jump, that'll be something!" He turned to Luke. "Of course, you don't have to."

"I wasn't planning on it."

"Doesn't surprise me," Tim said and turned to Tommy. "Are you surprised?"

"Nope."

Jo noticed Luke's hand tighten on the reins which

153

he loosened immediately when Silver tossed his head. She sensed he was angry by the way his eyes darkened, but his voice was steady when he spoke. "I didn't come here to argue. I thought we were going to have a nice, slow trail ride today."

"Yes," Amy chimed in. "Let's ride."

"But not slow," Carla said, "My horse needs to gallop."

Susan nodded. "So does mine."

"But Jo can't," Wendy replied.

"That's okay," Jo said quickly. "You guys go on ahead."

Carla looked at Susan and then at the twins. "We'll race you to the old oak tree by Olsen's pasture."

The twins glanced at each other and then at Jo.

"Oh, come on! She can catch up." Susan kicked her horse into a canter.

"Yeah, come on!" Carla echoed as she did the same. The twins shrugged and then raced down the yard road after the girls.

"Aren't you going too?" Jo asked Luke and Amy.

"We'll stay with you," Luke answered and then grinned. "Besides, these Arabians could beat their horses, no questions asked."

Amy giggled. "I hadn't thought about that."

"Yeah, well. No need to add fuel to the fire that's burning in those guys."

"That's true," Jo answered, "but I really don't know why Tim and Tommy act so mean sometimes."

Luke shrugged. "It's just the way some people are." He nudged Silver into a walk toward the main road. When they reached it, no one said a word. They just all turned their horses in the opposite direction from the one the twins had taken.

****

"I really wish Tim and Tommy would stop putting Luke down," Jo said to Wendy at breakfast the next day. She'd tried not to let the incident yesterday bother her, but it did.

"Yeah, I know," Wendy answered, "but Luke's cool about it."

Mary Anne yawned. "You can't change how people feel. Besides, Tim's a jerk."

"You didn't think so when you were dating him," Wendy said.

"Just shut up."

"You shut up."

"Girls." Aunt Viv frowned at them. "Stop arguing."

"She started it," Mary Anne replied.

"Did not."

"Did."

Their mother put her cereal spoon down with a clang that made both of them snap their mouths closed in surprise. "I said stop it. You're both acting like children. Any more arguing and I'll send you to your rooms like I did when you were in grade school. And no radios either. Do I make myself clear?"

"Yes, ma'am," Wendy replied.

"Sure," Mary Anne said and managed to stop herself from rolling her eyes.

Jo kept her gaze focused on her cereal. She'd never heard her aunt get angry before. Her leg must hurt more than she let on. Jo wondered if Aunt Viv was still taking the pain pills at night.

She felt guilty for having brought up the subject of Tim. It would've been smarter to wait and talk to Wendy

155

later when Mary Anne wasn't around. She had started coming down to breakfast instead of sleeping half the morning, although she usually didn't say much. Still, Jo knew her aunt liked having everyone at the table for meals.

Jo looked up from her bowl and glanced at Mary Anne. Had her cousin really cared about Tim? They'd dated for over a year. Mary Anne rarely came out of her room when the twins were here and never if Carla was present. It was probably hard for her cousin to see Tim with another girl. Jo could relate since she'd spent yesterday afternoon watching Amy with Luke. Not that they had actually flirted with each other, but it was still hard to be around them together.

So why had Mary Anne snuck out to see Bob? Jo was pretty sure that was who had left her off at the end of the yard road that night, although Jo didn't think he'd been by the past couple of weeks, probably because Mary Anne knew she'd been sleeping in the hammock.

Jo still hadn't told her aunt what she'd seen. She had no doubt Mary Anne would carry through on her threat to stir up trouble with Luke. But now that she was well enough to ride again, Aunt Viv had suggested she return to her regular bed, so Jo didn't know if Mary Anne would start up with Bob again. What would she do then?

In spite of the fact that Tim didn't like Luke, Jo wished Tim would like Mary Anne. Life was getting complicated and there wasn't a magic wand that Jo could wave to make everything right. She'd wished for that often enough after her parents died.

Jo sighed. Like her cousin had said, you can't change how people feel.

Chapter Fifteen

As Jo and Wendy approached the cabin later that afternoon, Jo was glad they'd had a chance to talk about Mary Anne on their walk over. "So you think maybe your sister still likes Tim?"

Wendy shrugged. "Maybe. She and Tim were arguing a lot just before Christmas. Carla was flirting with him a lot and I think Mary Anne was jealous. She wanted to go steady and he didn't."

"So he broke off with her?"

"I think he did, but I don't know. Mary Anne doesn't tell me much. She likes to keep secrets."

Jo felt a little guilty. She hadn't told Wendy about what she'd seen, so she was keeping a secret too. Maybe she should change the subject.

"When was the last time you were at the cabin?"

"Gosh, it's been months. With Mom breaking her leg, I had to do chores around the house after school and then the club likes to ride on Saturdays. Why?"

"No reason," Jo said, although she felt a sinking feeling in her stomach. Had Luke been coming here with Amy? "When I was here the last time, it looked like someone had been using the place."

"Really?" Wendy asked and opened the door to step inside. She looked around. "You're right. Someone has been here."

"Maybe Luke?" Jo tried to sound casual. "You guys

used to come here."

"I doubt it. He played varsity baseball this spring and the team practiced every afternoon. Since school's been out, he's been helping his dad in the fields."

"When does he find time to date Amy?" As soon as the words were out, Jo wanted to bite her tongue. She hadn't meant to ask that.

"I guess Saturday nights. That's usually date night around here." Wendy gave her a curious glance. "Are you interested in Luke?"

Jo felt her face flame. "No! I mean…well, I like him as a friend. He…he's always been really nice to me." That sounded pretty lame, even to her, and she hoped Wendy wouldn't start teasing her. To her surprise, Wendy looked thoughtful.

"You know, Luke is nice to you. Oh, he's *nice* to everyone and lots of girls think he's really cute, but he pretty much stays to himself. I think Amy's the first girl he's really dated."

"Amy is pretty and she's friendly, so I guess it's not surprising," Jo forced herself to say.

"Yeah, she's really popular. When she moved here, lots of guys asked her out, but I think she had her eye on Luke right from the beginning. I think they had most of their classes together."

Jo tried to ignore the pang that flashed through her. Amy was in the same grade as Luke. Middletown was a small school. There weren't that many choices, at least not for English and math and history. "So they hit it off right away?" Jo blurted before she could stop herself.

"I don't know. Mary Anne said Amy asked Luke to the Sadie Hawkins dance at Valentine's, and then Amy had a party a couple of weeks later. Mary Anne and I both went and Luke was there. Amy pretty much hung around him all night. After that, everyone pretty much figured they were dating."

"But you don't know for sure?" Jo clamped a hand over her mouth. Why couldn't she stop asking stupid questions?

Wendy's eyes widened. "Oh, my gosh! You do like Luke!"

"No! I mean—"

"You do! I can tell!" Wendy shook her head. "I don't know what to say. Luke took Amy to prom and the Memorial Day picnic. They spend time riding. Maybe she likes him more than he does her. Luke still has his class ring, so they aren't going steady, if that helps."

Jo forced a smile. "It's not like I can do anything about it."

"You never know." Wendy grinned, looking less serious. "Luke did ask a lot about you while you were gone, and he always asks how you are. I haven't heard him do that with anyone else, not even Amy."

A small ray of hope sprang up inside Jo with those words. Could it be true? Luke did like her a little more than other girls? Even—maybe—Amy? Did Jo dare hope?

"What's that song you like so much?" Wendy asked. "The one by Doris Day?"

Jo smiled. " '*Que Sera Sera*.' What will be, will be."

Maybe, just maybe, the future would be bright after all.

Que sera.

****

"How about walking down to the river?" Jo asked Wendy a couple of days later when they'd gotten bored with board games. "I love the sound of the water, and I didn't get to experience it that day I got scared and ran away."

'Um, I don't know if we should. It might not be safe."

"Why wouldn't it be safe? It's only four o'clock. There shouldn't be anyone partying or drinking down there at this hour." Secretly, Jo hoped maybe Luke would be fishing since he hadn't been by since Saturday, but she didn't want it to look like she was chasing him.

"It's not that. But we don't know who's been using the cabin."

"Probably just someone who went fishing or something."

Wendy shook her head. "I didn't see any fishing poles, did you?"

"No, but maybe whoever it was took his gear with him. It's not like we're living in a high crime rate area."

"Well, not like New York, for sure," Wendy replied, "but since the casino opened last year, there have been some incidents of stolen cars and a few break-ins even."

"But the casino is thirty miles away."

"Mom says people come to gamble from all over the state. If they lose a lot of money, they might be desperate."

"Maybe, but why would they go to the river?"

Wendy hesitated before answering. "Maybe because they *are* desperate." She looked away. "Maybe they feel down, like you do sometimes."

Jo felt her eyes widen in shock. "You still think I went to the river because I wanted to drown myself?"

Wendy shook her head quickly. "I don't want to think that. Most of the time, you seem to be okay. I know how hard it was when my dad died, though. It took me a long time to feel good about anything."

Jo nodded. "It isn't easy. I miss my parents a lot, but '*Que Sera Sera*' was my mom's favorite song. That's why I like it. She always told me that no matter how bad today turned out to be, tomorrow was another day." Jo smiled, remembering. "Well, I think she got that line from *Gone With The Wind*. That was her favorite book."

"I saw the movie." Wendy furrowed her brow. "But it didn't turn out good. Scarlett didn't get Rhett. He left her all alone."

"Maybe. Mom said Scarlett never gave up hope, no matter how bad times were. First the war, then almost losing her home, then her mother…" Jo's voice trailed off and she blinked back tears, forcing a little smile instead. "Anyway. I think Scarlett will get Rhett back. She's got time on her side."

Wendy giggled. "Like in the Stones song?"

"Something like that." Jo hoped she had time on her side with Luke, too, but that was a different story. She folded the play board, put it aside, and stood. "Come on. Let's go down to the river and listen to the water. I promise I won't jump in."

"You'd better not," Wendy answered, but her eyes were twinkling.

****

They'd gotten waylaid by Mary Anne on their way out. She'd wanted to know where they were going. Wendy gave Jo a conspiratorial look. "Just for a walk," she said. Mary Anne had looked suspicious, but she hadn't asked anything else.

The walk to the river took a little longer than Jo remembered, but maybe that was because she had been running like demons were chasing her the last time. And maybe they were—her own private demons of loss. Her parents. Losing Luke—well, not actually, of course. Jo chided herself. Luke had never been hers. He was a friend who had a girlfriend—or maybe not as much of a one as she'd thought?

"What are you thinking about?" Wendy asked.

Jo was glad the trees lent shade to the path so Wendy wouldn't see how red her face probably was. She couldn't tell her cousin she'd been daydreaming about Luke again. She'd already said too much. "Oh, nothing really. Why?"

"You were frowning so hard I thought you were trying to solve all the problems on the news."

Jo almost laughed. If she'd been frowning, then at least Wendy wouldn't catch on to her real thoughts. Thoughts that were confusing. "I doubt fifteen-year-old girls could do much about the news…unless you count screaming at Beatles' concerts."

"They're coming to Minneapolis in August," Wendy said, accepting the change in subject. "I sure wish Mom would let us go."

"They're probably already sold out."

"Probably." Wendy sighed. "I sure would like to see Paul, though. He's so cute."

"He is but, you know, I've always liked John."

"Yeah, but he's married."

Wives. Girlfriends. Maybe there was something wrong with her. "George and Ringo are cute too."

"Yeah." Wendy giggled. "Or maybe I should say 'yeah, yeah, yeah' like they do in *She Loves You*."

Not a good title for Jo to think about. Did Amy love Luke? She'd only known him a few months. But then, she had asked him to the Sadie Hawkins dance. How serious were they?

"You're frowning again."

"Sorry." Jo pushed her confusing thoughts aside and changed the subject. "I can hear the water running over the rapids. We should be almost there."

"Almost."

They walked the rest of the way in silence, the sound of the water growing louder as they wound their way along the twisted trail. Dead leaves from last winter crunched under their feet while new undergrowth brushed against their legs.

"Here we are," Wendy said as they passed the last few trees and came to the grassy bank of the rapidly flowing river. "Do you want to sit down?"

Jo's gaze took in the opposite bank where she'd seen Luke fishing. She realized she'd been hoping he'd be there again, but the area was empty. Still, the last time he'd appeared from nowhere, it seemed. Maybe there was a different path over there?

"Let's go sit on those boulders."

Wendy gave her a surprised look. "They're on the other side."

"Well, there's a bridge over there."

"It's pretty rickety."

Luke had crossed it when he ran after her. "Maybe for horses," Jo said, "but it looks solid enough for people."

"I don't know. Lots of the boards are out. People have gotten hurt."

"Probably because they weren't careful," Jo answered. "It's not like it's really haunted. That's just a legend."

"I don't think—"

"Phooey." Luke had crossed it. It had to be safe. Besides, Jo wanted to see what was over there. "Look." She pointed to some trash and empty beer cans by the foot of the bridge. "This is where those kids must come to party."

Wendy looked uncertain. "All the more reason for us to go home."

"It's still light. No one is going to come here to party until after dark. We'll be home by then." Jo started walking toward the bridge. "Come on. Let's explore a little."

"They're just a bunch of rocks," Wendy grumbled as she followed behind. "That ridge is probably an Indian mound. We have them in lots of places."

"You're probably right," Jo said as she continued on. She really didn't know why she was so obsessed with checking the other side, except that Luke had appeared from nowhere. It was silly of her to think he'd just pop up again, but she couldn't let it go.

As they crossed the bridge, it swayed precariously. Jo stepped carefully over the missing planks and took care to stay in the middle since most of the railings had given way as well. She didn't want to admit that Wendy was probably right. The bridge was in really bad shape. Did Luke use it regularly?

Jo let out the breath she'd been holding when she finally stepped off onto solid ground. Wendy followed, looking none too happy.

"Don't ask me to go back that way."

Jo furrowed her brow. "Then how are we going to get home? Wade across the rapids?"

Wendy shook her head. "The rocks drop off

suddenly and the water is really deep in the middle. Plus, the current is too fast."

"Well, then, we have to cross the bridge."

"Nope. There's a newer one about a mile farther down. We'll take it."

That was probably the way Luke had come. There were trees on this side too, although they weren't as thick. Had he stepped out from behind one when Jo spotted him? She thought she'd have noticed. She walked over to the boulders. Up close, they were huge and loosely piled on top of one another. Jo started to climb.

"What are you looking for?" Wendy said, not budging from her spot.

She could hardly say Luke—or at least, where he had come from last time. "You said this is an Indian mound?"

"No. The ridge—the ground beneath those rocks— might be a mound. Maybe not. We've got lots of hills around here. Come on down. We need to get home."

"Just a sec." Jo had reached a small ledge and wedged herself around one of the boulders. Then she stopped in surprise at a gaping hole on the other side. "There's a cave here!"

"Great. Probably some animal lives in it. Let's go."

"Just one more minute." Jo hunched down to peer inside. The opening wasn't very big and was really more of flat slate-like rock propped up by boulders on either side. It was too dark inside to see if the cave went deeper, but she did notice a couple of fishing poles, along with a net and bucket just inside the cave's entrance. Probably Luke's. With the entry hidden, that would explain how he'd suddenly appeared out of nowhere.

Cynthia Breeding

"Come on!" Wendy shouted. "We've got a couple of miles to walk before it gets dark. Mom will ground us for sure."

Jo took one last look and sidled around the rocky ledge and climbed back down to where Wendy waited.

She'd have to explore the cave another time.

Chapter Sixteen

Jo looked at the red, white, and blue bunting on the picnic tables and thought how different this year's Fourth of July celebration seemed from the last time she was here. The tables still held many different kinds of potato salad and various "Hot Dish" recipes along with homemade pies and cakes, but the atmosphere was changed.

A cacophony of sound blared from transistor radios near the sandy strip of shoreline where a bunch of the high school kids were gathered. From the discord, it sounded like a competition between the British rock groups and the older American standbys, with a little bit of country music thrown in. But that wasn't what caught Jo's attention.

In addition to the usual family sedans and dusty pickups, the graveled parking space beside the lake also held an assortment of low-rider cars sporting lots of chrome and no mufflers. At least that's what it sounded like when one of them drove up. Their drivers had slicked-back hair—which Jo supposed was what Wendy called greaser-style—and congregated around their cars, occasionally revving an engine to compete with several motorcycles that circled the lot. Those riders wore leather vests and had their hair tied back in ponytails.

"Who are those people?" Jo asked Wendy as they set Aunt Viv's prize pies on an already overloaded table.

Wendy grimaced. "Two of the guys by the cars are Ken and Frank…they're the ones from Minneapolis that Mary Anne thinks are so sophisticated. I think the other cars belong to kids whose dads work at the plant too."

"What about the motorcycles?"

"I'm not sure. They started showing up on weekends last summer, right after the casino opened. Most of them left in August to go to a bike rally in South Dakota, so I suppose they will again this year."

"They're not from here?"

Wendy shook her head. "I think they drive up from the cities. A lot of casino workers are from there. Oh, oh," she said, switching subjects, "there's Mary Anne. She's going to be in so much trouble if Mom sees her!"

Jo turned in the direction Wendy was looking. Mary Anne had joined Ken and Frank by the cars. An extra button on her Madras shirt was undone, but it was her khaki skirt that made Jo raise her eyebrows in disbelief. Mary Anne must have rolled the skirt six inches at the waist because half her thighs were bared. "Holy cow! Why would she dress like that?"

"Her friend, Ruby." Wendy pointed to the girl who had walked up to the group. "Mary Anne thinks she's cool."

Jo blinked. She'd thought Mary Anne wore too much makeup, but Ruby looked like the English models with raccoon eyes. Her hair was bleached almost white and cut really short. Unlike those models, though, Ruby was curvy everywhere. A halter top exposed her midriff as well as practically all of her breasts, and the shorts she wore looked more like a bathing suit bottom. As Jo watched, several boys moved away from their cars to surround Mary Anne and Ruby.

"Your mom is going to be really mad."

"If she sees Mary Anne," Wendy answered. "Remember Mom was going to stop off at the nursing home and leave some pies. She'll visit a few of the folks there before she comes over. By that time, those guys will be gone and Mary Anne will roll her skirt down."

"She won't go with them?"

"I don't think so. She knows Mom is expecting to see her here."

Jo hesitated, then decided she would tell Wendy about Mary Anne sneaking out. Before she could, though, another car honked and Wendy grabbed her hand. "Come on. It's Tim and Tommy."

Jo followed her cousin to where the twins had parked their car—a brand new convertible—on the opposite end of the parking area. "Nice car," she said as Tim and Tommy and their girlfriends piled out. "Did you just get it?"

"Two days ago. Dad surprised us." Tommy held open the door. "Take a look inside."

"Better yet, do you want to go for a ride?" Tim asked.

"We just got here." Carla took Tim's arm.

"Yeah." Susan put her hand on Tommy's shoulder. "I'm starving."

Jo didn't need the annoyed looks the girls gave her to get the picture. "Maybe some other time."

"Just let us know," Tim said as Tommy nodded, which caused both girls to narrow their eyes at Jo.

She turned away, wishing she could tell both of them their boyfriends were safe—at least from her. She wasn't interested in either Tim or Tommy. The guy she was interested in hadn't put in an appearance. Jo didn't know whether to be relieved or disappointed that Luke wasn't there.

And then she caught her breath. Luke must have parked behind the group of low-riders, for he was walking their way, Amy by his side.

****

Jo lay back in the hammock and gazed at the stars twinkling like diamonds on a black velvet sky. The town's fireworks had long been over and everyone had gone home. She'd waited until her aunt and cousins had gone to bed before coming down and going outside. Jo welcomed the silent peacefulness of the night in contrast to the noisy, chaotic day it had been. She hadn't taken much notice of the clashing sounds of various music stations from the small beach, nor had she been overly concerned when a fight nearly broke out between one of the low-riders and a guy on a motorcycle. The county constable, who had been about to take a slice of apple pie, quickly put an end to that disruption. The bikers had driven off toward Giddesberg and the low-riders had revved their engines—probably to compete with the noise from the bikes—and had driven off in another, leaving Ruby and Mary Anne behind.

By the time Jo's aunt arrived, Mary Anne had rolled her skirt down to its regular length, but Aunt Viv hadn't been pleased to see her talking to Bob. He had scowled and walked off when Aunt Viv summoned Mary Anne to help her, and Mary Anne had sulked for the rest of the afternoon.

Even after two children chasing a dog had plowed into the potato salad table, splattering Jo and the ground in a mayo-mess, she'd managed not to get upset. They were little kids, after all.

Luke and Amy were a different matter. They'd joined the group by the convertible, and Jo wasn't sure which bothered her most—the near glares from the twins' girlfriends or Amy's super-friendliness. Either way, it was hard for Jo to respond. She'd had to endure standing behind Amy in the food line while Luke asked her what she'd like and filled her plate for her. And then, when Amy opted to sit on the grass rather than at one of the benches, Luke had taken off his jacket and put in on the ground for her. Wendy plopped herself down beside them and Jo had little option but to do the same, although she'd lost her appetite and could barely choke down the small portion of Hot Dish she'd served herself. Luke had asked her if she was feeling all right and she'd nodded, because what could she say? No?

Jo closed her eyes, hoping the gentle swaying of the hammock would lull her to sleep like it had before, but her mind was in turmoil. Had Luke just been acting like a gentleman this afternoon, or did he really think Amy was special? Jo was pretty sure Amy felt that way about Luke, but then, so did she. Why had Luke asked her if she felt all right? Maybe he was just being a gentleman when he asked? She shouldn't care. Jo opened her eyes and looked up at the sky. She needed to stop replaying the picnic scene in her mind.

Slowly she became aware of a car idling at the end of the yard road. A few minutes later she heard footsteps crunching on the gravel. Mary Anne? Jo lay still, thoughts of bikers and low-riders and drinking parties down by the river fleetingly passing though her head. Maybe she shouldn't have come outside after all. Then she grimaced at letting her imagination run wild.

Jo turned slightly in the hammock as the footsteps

drew nearer and wasn't sure if she was relieved or not to see Mary Anne rounding the corner of the house, heading for the back door. Her cousin didn't look in the direction of the hammock, but then, why would she? Jo had taken to sleeping in the house since her rib healed. She watched as Mary Anne disappeared inside the house.

Jo lay back in the hammock, staring into the night. She didn't want to tattle on her cousin, but this was the second time she'd caught Mary Anne sneaking in. Aunt Viv needed to know, but first maybe Jo should talk to Mary Anne. That kind of felt like the right thing to do.

That's what she'd do.

****

Jo hesitated in front of Mary Anne's door the next morning. It was barely past dawn and her cousin wouldn't be happy to be awakened this early, but Jo wanted to talk to her before Aunt Viv got up. This was the best time. Taking a deep breath, Jo knocked softly. When she didn't get an answer, she knocked again, hoping Wendy wouldn't hear her, next door. When there was still no answer, Jo turned the knob slowly and stepped inside, stopping to let her eyes adjust to the dim light beginning to come through the window. Muttering, Mary Anne turned over, pulling the covers over her head.

Jo glanced around the room. The place was a mess with clothes and shoes strewn everywhere. Makeup littered the dresser top. Some of the contents of Mary Anne's purse had spilled from where she'd tossed it in a chair beside the door. Jo was surprised to see a package of cigarettes and leaned to pick up the pack. When had her cousin started smoking?

"Leave that alone!"

Startled, Jo dropped the pack and turned. Mary

Anne was sitting against the headboard glaring at her. "I—"

"What are you doing in my room?"

"I need to talk to you."

"About what?"

Jo drew a breath. "About last night. I saw you coming in."

Mary Anne narrowed her eyes. "You were spying on me?"

"No! I…I couldn't sleep, so I went out to the hammock."

"You're like major weird, you know? Who sleeps in a hammock?"

"It's comfortable. I like it."

"Hmmm." Mary Anne gave her a speculative look. "Maybe you were outside because *you* were waiting for someone."

"No! Why would I be—"

"Maybe Luke?" Mary Anne asked. "I know you have a crush on him."

Jo felt her cheeks warm. Was she that obvious to everyone? Maybe even Luke? She felt her face heat even more. She'd just die of embarrassment if he knew. "He's got a girlfriend."

"Oh, yeah. Miss Mary Poppins. Pure as the driven snow." Mary Anne swung her legs over the side of the bed and went over to the dresser to pick up her hairbrush. "I'll bet Luke hasn't even gotten to first base with her yet."

"First base?"

"You know."

"Know what?"

Mary Anne laid down the brush and stared at her.

"Oh, my God. You *don't* know, do you? First base is…well, let's just say it involves heavy necking and petting."

Jo was pretty sure her face was on fire. If she touched it, she'd burn her fingers. She didn't want to think about Luke and Amy kissing or…touching like that. She didn't even want to think of them holding hands. "Nice girls don't do stuff like that."

"You're probably right." Her cousin shrugged. "Maybe you should do Luke a favor—do yourself one, too—and tell him to meet you at that hidden cabin."

Jo remembered how Mary Anne had tried to get her into trouble two years ago with a forged note to meet Luke at the cabin, but she was still shocked to hear Mary Anne suggest such a thing for real. "I would never—"

"No, you probably wouldn't. Actually, it would be a pretty nice place to go with a guy. Private and all that."

Jo felt her mouth gape. The cabin had been used recently. "Do you…did you…have you gone there? With a boy?"

Mary Anne gave her a wide-eyed look. "Me? Are you saying I'm not a nice girl?"

"No. Of course not. I mean… Aunt Viv would be really upset if she thought you were doing something like that."

Mary Anne gave Jo a sly smile. "If you tell Mom you saw me out last night, I'll say I was the one who couldn't sleep and saw you from my window. You and Luke were in the hammock."

"That's a lie!"

"It is? Prove it." She walked to the door and opened it. "You better go or you'll be late for breakfast. I wouldn't want to have to say you look really tired…if you get my drift. Mom might get suspicious. Of *you*."

"But—"

"And don't say anything about the cigarettes either, if you know what's good for you. Get it?" Mary Anne gave her shove. "Go."

Jo opened her mouth to protest, but her cousin had already shut the door. Jo turned away, more confused than ever about what she should do. She didn't have any proof. Mary Anne would just turn around everything Jo said. Luke would get blamed for something he didn't do. What if her aunt believed Mary Anne—she was her daughter, after all—and Jo was just an orphan. What if Aunt Viv went to talk to Luke's dad?

She would die of embarrassment if that happened. She really, truly would.

****

Mary Anne shot Jo a warning look when they assembled at the breakfast table an hour later, but Jo tried her best not to look her cousin in the eye. Instead, she poured milk on her cereal. Wendy kept up a constant chatter about which events the riding club was going to participate in at the county fair, so Jo was spared the need to keep up a conversation. Aunt Viv seemed unusually quiet and Jo wondered if she'd slept well. She looked tired, or maybe troubled.

"I can't wait to beat those kids from the Raiders club," Wendy said. "Tommy says if we really practice hard, we can do it."

Mary Anne sniffed. "If you spend any more time with horses, you might as well sleep in the barn. You already smell like you do."

"Don't put down your sister," Aunt Viv said. "There's nothing wrong with working hard and achieving goals."

"I'm just saying I like to smell clean. So do my friends."

"Oh, yeah. Poking their noses under the hoods of cars and having greasy hands is clean all right," Wendy said.

"You stop bickering too," Aunt Viv added. "Why can't you two get along? Honestly, I don't know what went wrong. I tried to raise each of you the same."

Mary Anne frowned. "What does that mean? That I'm not good enough?"

"I didn't say that."

"Just because Wendy acts like Miss Goody-Two-Shoes doesn't mean she is."

Wendy glared at her sister. "At least, I don't hang around with hoodlums."

"My friends aren't hoodlums!"

"They look like it."

"*Girls*," Aunt Viv began and then stopped as the back door opened and Luke stuck his head through. She managed a smile. "Come in, dear."

Luke stepped in and glanced around as if sensing something was wrong. Jo tried to keep her face impassive, although her heart skittered at the sight of him. Still, after what Mary Anne had said earlier, Jo didn't dare look too pleased to see him. "We didn't hear you ride up."

"I drove, since I have to go to town and pick up some grain." Luke laid a newspaper on the table. "I didn't know if you'd seen this. There's been a break-in."

"A break-in? Good heavens! Where?" Aunt Viv asked as she unfolded the paper.

"The municipal liquor store," Luke replied. "The

front window was smashed. It looks like whoever did it got away with only a few bottles and some cigarettes."

"Smashing the front window isn't very smart," Wendy said. "The liquor store is right on Main Street."

Mary Anne sharpened her gaze. "Did anyone see anything?"

Luke shook his head. "Not really. It was after midnight, and the only person loitering on the street was old Mr. Gustafson…and he was pretty drunk."

"That poor man needs to get some help," Aunt Viv said.

"Still, did he notice anything?" Jo asked.

"Mr. Gustafson said he heard a noisy engine, like a car with no muffler."

"Like the cars those low-riders drive?" Wendy smirked at Mary Anne. "Maybe one of your friends did it."

"*Enough*," Aunt Viv said.

"You can't take anything that old man says seriously," Mary Anne said dismissively. "Half the time he sees things that aren't even there."

"He didn't say he saw something. He said he heard it," Wendy argued.

Aunt Viv lifted an eyebrow. "Did you not hear me?"

Wendy slumped in her chair. "Yes, ma'am."

Mary Anne smiled and stood. "I think I'll just freshen up and go into town to see what I can find out."

"Actually, you won't be going to town," Aunt Viv said.

"Why not?"

"Because I think it's time you and I had a little talk—and right now would be a good time."

Chapter Seventeen

Wendy lingered after her mother's remark, saying she needed something from her bedroom, but Jo could feel Mary Anne's glare piercing her back as she and Luke made a hasty exit out the door toward the stables. She was certain Mary Anne thought she'd tattled to Aunt Viv about last night.

And she almost wished she had, since she was feeling guiltier by the minute. Mary Anne had snuck out last night and she'd had cigarettes in her purse. She was too young to buy them, so how had she gotten them? And she'd acted kind of drunk the time before, too. Where was she getting liquor? Jo worried her lip again. Did her cousin know who had broken in?

"You look like you're trying to solve the world's problems," Luke said.

"Just thinking about the break-in."

"Don't worry. They'll get caught."

"It's just…things seemed so safe when I was here year before last."

Luke nodded. "There have been changes since the casino was built and the manufacturing plant expanded. Folks have moved out here from the Twin Cities, and lots of strangers pass through, especially on the weekends. The city council calls it progress. The sheriff calls it something else." Luke shrugged. "Dad says you can't stop some things from happening."

Jo looked down at the ground, blinking back tears that suddenly sprang to her eyes. "Yeah, I know."

"God, I'm stupid." Luke placed a hand on her shoulder. "I'm sorry. I didn't think about your parents."

The warmth from his hand spread across her back like a comforting blanket and Jo felt her tension ease. "It's okay. I know I can't change what happened. It's just hard to remember they're really gone."

"I miss my mom too."

"Oh, jeepers. I should have thought about that."

"It's okay," Luke said. "She's been gone almost nine years, but I still think about her. Dad does too."

Jo nodded. "Mom used to say people you love will always live in your heart."

He rubbed her shoulder gently before dropping his hand. "You had a smart mom."

"Yeah, she was pretty cool."

"Who's pretty cool?" Wendy asked as she ran up to them with an unneeded sweater in her hand. Jo supposed that's what she'd wanted to get from her bedroom.

"Jo's mom," Luke said.

Wendy grimaced. "Well, my mom is steaming hot. She just grounded Mary Anne for two weeks! Not even phone calls!"

Jo felt her eyebrows raise about as high as they could go, her eyes wide open. "Were you listening?"

"Of course. From the stairs."

"But that's not nice."

Wendy seemed unaffected. "I wanted to know what Mom was so mad about."

Jo knew she shouldn't ask, but she did anyway. "And?"

"She told Mary Anne she knew about her sneaking

out and that it was going to stop. And, she's never to go riding in Bob's car again. Ever."

"Ummm…did your Mom tell Mary Anne how she found out?"

Wendy shook her head. "Mom never tells us how she finds out things. She just said she knew."

Jo had a sinking feeling in the pit of her stomach that felt as though she'd swallowed a rock. She hadn't tattled on her cousin, but Mary Anne would think she had.

…*if you know what's good for you*. Those were her cousin's last warning words to Jo this morning.

Would Mary Anne make trouble about Luke?

****

Jo didn't have much time to ponder on the situation because the sound of horses cantering up the yard road diverted everyone's attention. The twins yanked their horses to a sudden stop, spewing gravel in all directions.

Luke frowned. "You'll damage their mouths doing that."

"We're using snaffle bits." Tim looked down from the saddle at Luke. "I assume you know they flex?"

Luke held his gaze level. "The sides of their mouths will get tough anyway."

"I think we can handle our own horses," Tim replied as Carla and Susan trotted up behind them and cut off the conversation.

"Anyway, we're here to practice jumping," Tommy said. "The fair is only a month away, and we need the practice."

Luke followed Jo and Wendy into the barn while the others moved into the paddock to set the bars. He knit his brows as Jo brought an English saddle from the tack room. "How's Flame doing with that?"

180

"She's remembering it from two years ago, I think," Jo answered. "I suppose it feels better than the heavy Western one."

'Probably." Luke spread the blanket over the mare's withers and then took the saddle from Jo. "I just don't like the idea of your jumping her. She's not a hunter like Jupiter."

"Flame's catching on quick." Wendy brought the gelding out of his stall. "And Jo's getting a lot better too."

"You're sticking to the low jumps?" Luke asked.

"For now," Jo answered, "but I really want to learn the in-and-out."

"That's a really hard jump. The horse has only a stride between the two bars. If she doesn't land right, you'll both tumble." Luke rubbed his hand along Flame's hind quarter. "I don't know she's ready for that."

"Are you guys coming out of there?" Tommy shouted.

"Coming!" Wendy replied as they led their horses out. "What's the rush?"

"Tim wants us to practice riding in a circle like we'll do as an exhibition." Tommy pointed to the paddock. "We've set the jumps like they'll be at the fair."

Jo looked at the circle. The first jump was low and the next one a foot higher, but she'd done both of those before. Then came the triple bar and, finally, the in-and-out.

"Everyone line up." Tim trotted over to the fence. "I'll go first. Once my horse has cleared the second jump, Carla can follow. Everyone leave two jumps between horses."

"I'll ride last," Jo said, "since I haven't practiced the last two."

"No time like now to start," Tim answered.

"Flame isn't ready for those." Luke hooked his thumbs into his belt loops.

"How's the mare ever going to get trained if Jo doesn't try the jumps?" Tim replied. "We want everyone to be in top form when we do the exhibition."

Luke shifted his weight slightly. "There's no sense in putting either horse or rider in danger."

Tim jutted his jaw. "Why don't you leave that up to Jo to decide? It's not like she's your girl and you can tell her what to do."

The words slammed home hard to Jo, removing any warm, fuzzy traces lingering from Luke's rubbing her shoulder earlier. It had meant nothing. He had a girlfriend.

Luke raised an eyebrow. "Are you in the habit of telling Carla what to do?" he asked Tim.

Tim glanced over to where Carla and Susan were huddled together talking. "What she can't hear won't hurt her."

"Aw, come on, Tim," Tommy said. "The girls are already giving us dirty looks."

Jo looked at the girls, who were definitely glaring at *her*. What did they think? That she was flirting with the twins? If only they knew she could barely tolerate Tim, and Tommy was too much of a prankster for her taste. "You guys get started. I'll do the first two jumps and then ride around the last two."

"Whatever." Tim spun his horse around, gesturing for Tommy to follow. "But I don't want us to lose points at the show."

"Don't worry. There's plenty of time yet." Wendy mounted Jupiter and trotted into the paddock to get in line.

Luke cupped his hands to give Jo a leg up and then he took hold of a rein. "Regardless of what Tim says, there's nothing that says you have to do the exhibition."

"But I'll let them down."

"Winning is not everything," Luke said.

"But—"

"Are you coming or not?" Tim yelled.

"I'd better go."

Luke released the rein. "Just don't try the in-and-out until you and Flame are both ready, okay? I don't want you getting hurt."

He looked so serious that a warm glow spread over Jo. It sounded like Luke cared—probably as much for the horse—but he cared. At least, a little.

Jo gave him a big smile. "Okay."

****

Wendy brought the mail from their roadside mailbox into the kitchen two days later, just before lunch. Handing Mary Anne a copy of *Seventeen*, Wendy turned to Jo. "You got a letter."

"A letter? Who—"

"Don't know." Wendy put the rest of the stack down on a chair and handed the envelope to Jo. "There's no return address."

"You shouldn't be checking other people's mail," Aunt Viv admonished.

"I was just curious."

"Maybe Rosalie wrote...no, it's postmarked here."

"Well, open it!" Wendy said.

Aunt Viv frowned. "Really, this isn't our business."

"It's okay," Jo answered as she tore the letter open. "I just wonder who would…" She stopped suddenly, feeling vaguely sick.

"What is it?" Her aunt moved a pot off its burner and hurried over to her. "You're white as a sheet."

The letter fluttered to the floor from Jo's trembling fingers. "It's…"

"It's what?" Aunt Viv bent down to pick it up. Her eyes widened as she read the brief message. "Who in the world would be so cruel?"

"What does it *say*?" Wendy asked impatiently.

Aunt Viv looked at Jo. "Do you want me to read it?"

Jo took a deep breath and nodded. "You might as well."

Her aunt looked down at the letter. "*Back off or leave.*"

"That's it?" Wendy asked.

"That's it."

"I don't get it." Wendy turned to Jo. "What are you supposed to back off of?"

"I don't know."

"But why would someone send this?"

Jo's first thought was Luke. He'd been really nice the other day, but Amy hadn't been there. Maybe someone had told her, though. Then, again, neither Carla nor Susan was very friendly. They had both glared at Jo on Saturday. And, of course, Mary Anne blamed her for being grounded. Jo's gaze shifted to her cousin, busily reading her magazine.

As if she felt Jo's eyes on her, Mary Anne looked up. "What?"

Jo hesitated. "Nothing."

Mary Anne's eyes narrowed. "Do you think I sent

that note?"

Jo felt her face get hot. The message was typed, as was the address on the envelope. She couldn't blame her cousin without proof. "No."

Aunt Viv looked at her daughter and then back to Jo. "Why would Mary Anne think you were blaming her?"

Jo glanced at Mary Anne. This was it then. The time for a decision. She caught the warning in her cousin's eyes and inhaled deeply before she turned to her aunt. "I was in the hammock the night of the Fourth of July because I couldn't sleep. I saw Mary Anne come in after midnight. Someone had dropped her off at the end of the driveway. She thinks I tattled on her."

"I see." Aunt Viv folded the letter and laid it on the table. "For your information, Mary Anne, I was also up that night. I couldn't sleep either, because I didn't take a pain pill. I was the one who saw you come in."

Mary Anne's face turned bright pink and she looked down at her plate. Jo couldn't tell if she was embarrassed or angry.

"And you, my dear," Aunt Viv said to Jo, "should have told me. I don't want either of my daughters or you holding things back. Don't worry about this letter. There will be no talk of you leaving us."

"Of course you're not leaving us," Wendy said. "Whoever wrote that is stupid."

Jo felt a tear trickle down her face and she wiped it away. "Thanks."

Aunt Viv patted her hand. "We are a family and you are a part of us now. You always will be." She glanced at Mary Anne. "Remember that."

Mary Anne shoved back her chair and stood. "Why should I? Maybe I don't want another sister!"

"I cannot believe you said that. Apologize."

"No."

Her mother's face blanched. "Then go to your room. *Now*."

Picking up her magazine, Mary Anne tossed her head and flounced out of the room without a backward look.

"Wow," Wendy said. "She's getting really mean."

"Mary Anne is going through a difficult time." Aunt Viv sighed. "She'll eventually come around." She gave Jo's hand another pat. "You are family now. I always want you to be truthful with me."

Jo nodded, more tears trickling down as guilt washed over her again. She hadn't told her aunt about the first time she'd caught Mary Anne out, and she hadn't mentioned the cigarettes. But doing so would make Mary Anne truly hate her.

She didn't want her cousin to hate her.

Chapter Eighteen

Jo turned up the volume on her transistor radio and placed it on her stomach as she lay in the hammock. Overhead, sunlight filtered through the trees, providing bits of warmth in the shade, but she hardly noticed.

Paul McCartney was singing "Yesterday" and—apart from the fact that she had received the hateful letter yesterday—the words seemed to hold special meaning for Jo today. Yesterday her troubles had seemed nonexistent, or at least not very important. Today, her world felt like it had been turned upside down.

Who had sent that letter? Who really disliked her that much?

She'd gone over all the possibilities a dozen times. Mary Anne had apologized this morning for her remark, but Jo was pretty sure Aunt Viv had made her do it and that Mary Anne didn't mean it. Her aunt had clarified that she was the one who had seen Mary Anne sneaking in, but that was after the letter had been mailed.

Wendy had told Jo last night that she thought Susan and Carla were jealous because Tim and Tommy didn't always pay that much attention to them, but the twins flirted with a lot of girls. When Jo had tentatively suggested maybe she was being too friendly with Luke and Amy didn't like it, Wendy had been so surprised her mouth dropped open. Amy wasn't like that, she'd said, and then added that Luke was friendly to everyone.

Like Jo needed to hear that. Or…maybe she did. Her feelings got all mixed up whenever she thought about Luke and, until yesterday, that had been her main concern.

Today, it hardly mattered, compared to the letter.

Worse, everyone was going to be here in a little while to practice the jumps again. Jo would have to face all of them, not knowing who had sent the letter.

Jo switched off the radio as "Do You Believe in Magic?" began playing. She could use a little magic in her life right now. If only she could be Jeannie from the TV program and blink everything all right. Or twitch her nose like Samantha. Jo sighed. Too bad magic didn't really happen. She slipped her legs over the side of the hammock and sat up. Maybe she couldn't change the way someone felt about her, but she could *act* like it didn't matter. She could pretend to be Emma Peel, saving the day for Mr. Steed…only Jo would do it by saving the day for the riding club. She'd make sure the Hill Riders would win at the horse show. "I'll show them. I'll be the best jumper of them all!"

With that determination, she set off toward the barn. The others would be here soon, but if they saw she was already practicing, they'd know she was serious about being part of the team. Maybe whoever sent the letter would see her differently then.

A short time later, Jo led Flame into the paddock and mounted. The jumps were still set as they had been last week. She cantered in a circle to let Flame warm up and then took the first two jumps and then did them once more. Jo eyed the last two. The triple bar didn't really look that hard. It was a wider jump than a single rail, but Flame had learned to stretch when she leapt. They should be able to clear it. Jo cantered around once more, then set the mare at the first three jumps. One. Two. The triple bar loomed ahead, looking bigger suddenly. She fought a moment of panic, remembering Luke's instructions to never tighten the reins before a jump. Then she felt Flame rise, the mare's powerful haunches sending them through the air. For a brief moment, it felt as though they were flying and then they touched down.

They'd done it! Cleared the triple bar without even a hoof nicking a rail. "Good girl!" Jo patted Flame's silky neck. "You know what to do, don't you?"

She heard horses coming up the yard road and eyed the in-and-out jump. She'd told Luke she wouldn't try it until she felt she and Flame were ready…but they'd just cleared the triple without a hitch. The in-and-out was really just two single jumps, close together. The riders had reached the yard. If they could see her doing *all* the jumps…

Once more, Jo circled, then tightened her knees and leaned over the withers. "We can do this, girl. Let's show 'em!"

Flame nickered and then moved forward, her gait collected. She picked up her hooves as gracefully as a ballet dancer, clearing the first two jumps easily and soaring over the triple as if she'd done it dozens of times. Jo inched forward a bit more, taking weight off the saddle and allowing the mare more freedom.

"No! Stop!"

Was that Luke's voice? Her attention diverted for a split second, she hitched the reins just as Flame rose for the first hurdle. It threw the mare off stride and she came down hard, falling to her knees, and sent Jo catapulting over her head.

For a brief moment, there was only space in front of Jo and then the ground came rushing up to meet her. She felt the heavy thud of the impact and the world went black.

****

Muted voices swirled through the fog of her brain as Jo drifted slowly toward the surface of consciousness. The sounds were varied—two soft and low, hardly discernible, like strains of music muffled behind a door. Another was higher-pitched and static-like, as though someone were crying and a third... the third was deeper and resonated. Jo recognized that voice.

She struggled to open her eyes and then quickly shut them against the glaring white light. One of the soft voices murmured something and the light dimmed. Cautiously, Jo opened her eyes again. Shapes swayed in front of her, dark and light, shifting like ghosts in a Halloween fun-house. One of those forms moved forward, coming into focus.

"Luke?"

"Yeah." He smiled and picked up her hand. "How do you feel?"

Jo squinted. "Dizzy. The room is spinning."

"That's natural," one of the soft voices said and Jo saw now that it was a nurse. "You've had a concussion. Things will stop moving around in a minute."

"Thank God you're awake." Aunt Viv hurried to the side of the bed. "I've been so worried."

"Me too." Wendy dabbed at her eyes with a wet handkerchief as she joined her mother and picked up Jo's other hand. "We thought you were dead."

"Wendy! We did not," Aunt Viv scolded, although her voice sounded shaky.

"But you said—"

"Never mind. Everything is going to be all right now."

Jo blinked as the room slowly stopped tilting and people were staying in one spot. She realized she was in a hospital room on an inclined bed. "What happened?"

"You had a bad fall from your horse," Aunt Viv said. "Do you remember that?"

"I...I remember riding in the paddock. I...was practicing some jumps, I think."

"Man, you jumped the triple!" Wendy exclaimed. "You started doing the in-and-out when—"

"We don't need all the details," Aunt Viv said. "It's enough that Jo remembers riding." She turned to the nurse. "Isn't that right?"

The nurse nodded. "She should recall all the details by and by. Right now, Jo should get some rest."

"Of course," Aunt Viv replied, herding Wendy toward the door. "We'll come back in a little while."

"Wait." Jo shifted a little, aware that Luke still held her hand and she was reluctant to let go. "I think I remember falling...shooting over Flame's head. Oh!" She clapped both hands over her mouth. "Flame fell! How badly is she hurt?"

"We don't know," Aunt Viv answered. "One of the twins called the vet. I rode in the ambulance with you."

"But Flame's going to be all right, isn't she?"

"She was standing when we left," Luke said, "so I don't think she broke a leg."

Jo stared at him, shocked. She knew what happened to horses with broken legs. "You don't *think*...?"

Luke shook his head. "We can't be sure until the doc takes an x-ray. She may have cracked something."

A crack could be as bad as a break, depending on where. "I'll never forgive myself if something happens to Flame," Jo whispered, more to herself than anyone.

"No. It's not your fault. It's mine." Luke sounded thoroughly miserable. "I yelled at you to stop. I should never have done that. It made you break your concentration." He looked down at the floor and then up at Jo, his eyes bright with unshed tears. "Can you forgive me? I know I don't deserve it, but—"

"You weren't at fault, Luke," Aunt Viv interrupted. "You did the right thing in trying to stop Jo from jumping. The timing was just off. There will be no more blame."

Luke kept his eyes fixed on Jo. "No more blame," she said and then shuddered.

It all came back clearly now. The jump, looming huge in front of her, Flame lifting her front legs just as Jo startled at the sound of Luke's voice. Flame struggling to stretch her neck against the tightening of the reins. The harsh click of the mare's back hooves hitting the rail. The rail crashing to the ground and then Flame falling forward… Jo began to tremble, recalling how totally powerless she had felt.

"That's enough for now," the nurse said firmly, shooing everyone to the door. "You get some rest. I'll bring back some broth shortly."

Jo nodded and watched as the door closed, leaving her alone. She wasn't at all hungry. How could she eat when her stomach was churning like river rapids? The realization that she could have been killed—and who knew what Flame's fate was—hit her harder than the ground had.

She wouldn't be jumping a horse again. Ever.

****

The hospital released Jo three days later with instructions to take things easy, and definitely no horseback riding for several weeks.

"But the county fair is in three weeks," Wendy protested as her mother drove them home. She'll miss the horse show!"

"So what?" Mary Anne asked from her corner of the back seat. "It's just a bunch of kids putting on an amateur show."

"What do you know about it?" Wendy shot back and then tapped Jo on the shoulder before her sister answered. "Do you think you'll be okay to ride by then?"

"I don't think Jo needs to worry about that right now," Aunt Viv replied. "The doctor said there was some brain swelling, and we aren't going to take any chances." She glanced toward Jo in the front seat. "I'm sorry, dear."

"It's okay." Secretly, Jo was relieved. She'd had nightmares every night over that last jump, seeing it get bigger and higher when those dreams came. The horse's hooves clipping the rail, the rail clattering down, and Jo's own heavy thud on the ground had all grown increasingly more vivid with each nightmare.

During the day, she'd started shaking when she thought about it. She didn't want to get anywhere near those jumps again.

"Well," Wendy grumbled from the back seat, "Flame needs to heal anyway."

Jo nodded. That the mare hadn't broken or cracked a bone was nothing short of a miracle. The vet had given her a thorough examination. Just like with a human being, the horse's knees had been bruised by the fall and she had strained tendons and pulled muscles, but nothing she wouldn't recover from. Despite Luke taking the blame for what happened, Jo wouldn't have forgiven herself if Flame had had to be put down. "I'm so glad she'll be all right."

"Me, too." Wendy bounced forward as they turned onto the yard road. "Oh, look! Everyone is waiting!"

Jo followed her pointed finger toward the barn, where the twins and their girlfriends stood, along with Luke and Amy. She cringed slightly at the sight of Amy.

Luke had come to the hospital each day in both the morning and the evening to check on Jo. She knew he was feeling guilty over the accident, but she still liked that he came to see her. He'd even brought her favorite raspberry swirl ice cream from the local creamery one night. The trouble was that Amy had visited Jo yesterday morning. She'd arrived just as Luke was leaving. There had been a slight frown on her face when she'd seen Luke there. It disappeared instantly and Jo wouldn't even have noticed it if she hadn't been watching like a hawk herself. Amy hadn't given any indication she was mad, though. She'd been as smiling and friendly as ever.

The group had ridden over and, as Jo got out of the car and walked toward them, it seemed to her the horses had all grown, too, and their hooves, stamping in the dust, were much larger, as well. Jo halted when Tim's horse bumped his rump into Tommy's gelding and that animal kicked out.

She'd never really thought about how dangerous a horse's hooves could be.

"Welcome back!" Amy came forward to give Jo a hug. "We're glad you're back."

"Yeah, us too," Tommy said while Susan and Carla

nodded.

"How soon before you can ride?" Tim asked.

"Not for several weeks," Jo answered.

"But the horse show—"

"She's not going to be able to ride in the horse show," Wendy said.

Luke grimaced and looked down at the ground. Jo knew immediately that he was feeling guilty about that too. "It's okay," she said. "Really. I'd probably just let the team down anyway. I can't jump as well as you." She didn't add that she planned never to jump again. Instead, she smiled brightly, pretending to be happy to be home.

Luke looked up, his eyes searching Jo's. It felt as though he were trying to read her mind. She felt her smile wavering. "Really," she said again. "I'm okay with not riding in the show." An expression she couldn't read crossed his face, but he let the subject drop.

"How about going into the barn to say hello to Flame?" Luke asked. "She's missed you."

Jo shook her head. She wasn't ready to see Flame yet. She wasn't quite sure why. She knew she felt guilty, but there was something else. Something she couldn't quite put a finger on. "I think I'll wait until tomorrow. I'm…I'm a little tired."

"Of course. You probably should rest," Amy said. "We just all wanted to come over to say we're glad you're okay."

"Well, while we're here, we may as well practice the jumps." Tim untied his horse from the rail. As he did, Tommy's gelding flattened his ears and nipped the horse's shoulder, causing him to squeal and kick back.

Jo jumped involuntarily, even though she was nowhere close to the animals. The strange expression crossed Luke's face again as he studied her, and Jo turned away before he could figure out what she was thinking.

She knew what the feeling was now. Fear.

Fear of the horses she had always loved.

****

"So let's go to the barn," Wendy said after breakfast the second morning Jo was home from the hospital. "I know you can't wait to see Flame!"

Jo stuck a spoonful of cereal into her mouth so she wouldn't have to answer. She had spent all day yesterday in her room, claiming she was really tired, but if she used that excuse again, Aunt Viv would start to worry and call the doctor. Even now, her aunt was watching her with a creased forehead and concern in her eyes. "Let me help with the dishes first."

"Don't bother about that," Aunt Viv said. "Just go and enjoy yourself."

"Yeah, come on!" Wendy added, pushing her chair away from the table. "Maybe you can't ride, but you can brush Flame anyhow."

"Just remember, the doctor said no bending over," Aunt Viv said as the girls walked to the door. "Let Wendy do the legs and hooves."

Jo nodded, only too glad to let Wendy see to the legs and feet. She knew her sudden fear of horses' hooves wasn't logical, but in her nightmares, they had become more and more dangerous.

She managed to hide her feelings as Wendy led Flame out of the stall and attached her lead to the hook on the wall. The mare suddenly seemed bigger too. Jo looked down at Flame's legs. "Is she really okay?"

"Yeah, pretty much. The farrier had to put special

shoes on her front hooves, but she'll be fine. "Here." Wendy handed Jo a brush and then frowned when Jo just stood there. "What's wrong?"

"Ah...nothing." Jo forced herself to step forward and put a tentative hand out. Flame turned her head, ears pricked forward, her velvety-brown eyes fixed on Jo. The mare bent her neck to gently blow across Jo's outstretched hand.

"See? I told you she missed you," Wendy said.

"Yeah." Jo slowly patted the horse's silky neck, reminding herself that Flame was her friend. The horse wasn't going to hurt her. She felt okay standing beside the mare, so maybe it was getting in the saddle and being afraid of falling off that got to her. Anyway, Wendy stood there with a curious look on her face and Jo forced herself to move forward and start brushing the mare's flank.

It didn't take very long to finish grooming, with Wendy helping her. Jo took the brushes back to the tack room, grateful to see Wendy had put Flame back in her stall when she returned.

"Mom's going to can dill pickles this morning," Wendy said. "Want to help?'

"Sure, but I don't know what to do."

"Don't worry. Mom does all the hard stuff."

The whole process was new to Jo and she found it fascinating. While Wendy went to the garden to pick the cucumbers, Jo washed dill stalks and watched her aunt prepare the pickling sauce and bring it to a boil. Once the cucumbers had been washed and sliced, Jo put them into sterile canning jars along with the dill and garlic cloves. Her aunt added a small chili pepper to each jar before pouring the cooled liquid over everything and sealing the jars with a rubber ring and metal cover.

"I had no idea so much was involved," Jo said as they cleaned up later. "My parents always bought everything at the store."

Aunt Viv smiled. "Well, you can do that, but I think home canning has better flavor. These will take several weeks before they're ready to eat, but meanwhile, there are some in the refrigerator we can have for lunch."

"I think I'll appreciate pickles a lot more after this."

"Wait until you taste Mom's canned peaches," Wendy said. "Yummy."

"I'll be picking up a crate of peaches for canning next week," Aunt Viv replied, "so you can both help with that."

"That'll be fun," Jo said.

"What will be fun?" Mary Anne asked as she came into the kitchen.

"Canning," Jo answered.

Her cousin gave her a look that clearly said she'd taken leave of her senses, but Jo didn't care. She'd had fun this morning and it took her mind off horses.

But horses found their way back into her thoughts right after lunch.

"The guys will be coming over this afternoon to practice jumps," Wendy said. "I know you can't ride, but you can watch and give us some pointers."

"I think I'll just lie in the hammock and read a book," Jo answered.

Wendy wrinkled her nose. "Books are for school."

"The doctor told me to take it easy, remember?"

"You won't strain yourself watching from the fence."

"If Jo wants to read a book, that's fine," Aunt Viv

responded, giving Wendy a stern look. "I don't want her to get overly excited."

"Stop being so bossy," Mary Anne added.

Wendy made a face at her sister and walked toward the door. "If you change your mind," she said to Jo, "you know where we are."

"Thanks."

Jo had no intention of joining the group, but she watched from the hammock as they arrived. Luke hadn't come today, so he must be working in the fields. Although it was early August, some crops would be ready. Jo settled into the hammock with a copy of Anya Seton's *Avalon*. Her mother had given the book to her as a Christmas present and Jo had put it aside, caught up in school activities. She hadn't felt like reading after the accident, but she hadn't packed the book away either.

Whether it was because the book was a last present from her mother and brought back sad memories or whether the laughter and the sounds of horses' hooves pounding the ground were interfering, Jo found she couldn't concentrate. After an hour in which she'd read only a few pages, she closed the book with a sigh.

What she needed to do was move. Sitting up slowly to avoid becoming dizzy, Jo swung her legs over the side of the hammock and stood. She decided to go for a walk. Maybe the solitude of the cabin would help.

Jo made her way through the trees, thinking how much easier the trail was to follow each time she took it and how much shorter the path seemed. The serenity of the woods, with her footsteps muffled on the soft dirt and songbirds in the trees, made her feel better immediately.

But that peace dissipated when she arrived at the cabin and opened the door. The place was in disarray.

Ashes spilled from the hearth. A blanket lay strewn half on the cot and half off. A dirty fork and dish along with a half-filled cup of cold coffee had been left on the table. On the counter by the sink sat a jar of peanut butter and half a loaf of bread in its polka-dot wrapper.

Someone had been using the cabin.

Jo backed out, closing the door behind her, not wanting to meet whoever had been occupying the cabin. She retraced her steps across the clearing and entered the woods, pausing when she came to the fork that led to the river. The sound of the rapids always soothed her. If she couldn't relax at the cabin, the river was her next choice.

She made her way down the winding trail, careful not to trip on roots or rocks. The last thing she needed was to fall, especially since Luke wouldn't be around to pick her up today like he had been the last time she had raced through the trees.

As though she had conjured him, when Jo stepped out of the woods onto the river's bank, she caught sight of Luke on the other side disappearing around the boulder leading to the cave. He must be getting the fishing poles he kept there.

What luck. Should she wait on this side until he reappeared? Or should she surprise him? He hadn't been by the house since the afternoon she came home, and she hadn't really had a chance to thank him for the hospital visits…

Jo walked toward the old bridge. It looked just as rickety as it had the last time she and Wendy were here, but Jo felt certain if she stayed away from the railing-less edge, she'd be fine. After all, Luke probably used it too.

Jo took a tentative step onto the first plank. It seemed sturdy enough. Slowly, she made her way forward, testing each board before she put her full weight on it. She was nearly midway when she heard an awful creaking sound and froze as the bridge began to sway beneath her. It groaned and moaned and, for a minute, Jo thought maybe the bridge was haunted by ghosts after all. She turned to run back just as the bridge gave one last grating sound and splintered.

With a shriek, Jo found herself hurled into cold water, the fast current sweeping her downstream.

Chapter Nineteen

Jo kicked her legs, struggling to break the surface before her breath ran out. Her jeans and sneakers held her down and she tried not to panic. She'd had swimming lessons and been taught about rip currents along Brighton and Coney Island beaches, but this was different. The strong current swept her along and there wasn't a way to swim perpendicular to it. Instead, it threatened to spin her, which would make her disoriented. Jo scissor-kicked hard, sputtering as her face finally emerged above water. She gulped air and then coughed when she swallowed water with it.

She managed to tread water while getting her bearings. At least the water wasn't cold, since it was August, but the river was deeper than she'd thought, given the rapids upstream of the old bridge. The river widened downstream. Jo flipped on her stomach, attempting to crawl toward the closer bank, but for every few inches of progress she made, the river seemed to pull her back. She'd wear herself out, at this rate. Should she just float?

Jo had just turned onto her back when she heard the soft thudding of horse's hooves along the narrow grassy north bank. She raised her head, hands sculling the water, and nearly cried with relief.

Silver Chief cantered parallel to the water, snorting as Luke wrapped the reins around the saddle horn and guided the stallion with his knees. He reached for the rope hanging by his knee.

"Try and catch this!" he shouted as he swung the loop.

The rope spun over the water, falling short. Jo tried reaching for it, only to have the water tug her in the other direction. She saw Luke's mouth move, but couldn't make out the words.

Time seemed to slow down. Jo saw Luke pull the rope back, but it appeared to creep along the surface. His hands also seemed to be in slow motion as he coiled the rope again for a second attempt. In her peripheral vision Jo became acutely aware that boulders closed in on the grassy bank, narrowing it abruptly.

Even as she thought it, she saw Silver Chief slide to a stop, half-rearing as Luke slid off and clambered onto the rocks. Jo made another attempt to turn against the current, windmilling her arms, but it had the effect of walking the wrong way on an escalator. Still, it held her in place...if only she could maintain the movement.

Luke reached a high point on one of the boulders that allowed him to swing the lasso over his head. It snaked out over the water once more, splashing the surface only a few feet from Jo. She kicked hard, trying to move forward. Her fingers grazed the rope before it slipped past her. Exhausted, she made one more effort, this time managing to wrap a hand around the line.

"Hang on!" Luke called as he slid down the rough, granite surface, keeping the rope taut at the same time. "Try and get both hands on it."

Jo's arms felt like lead. She wasn't sure how much strength she had left. She could feel her grip slipping.

"Hang on, Jo. Hang on! You can do it!"

Somehow, she did. Whether it was Luke's voice that gave her power or his intense gaze, holding her focused like a lighthouse beam, she didn't know. She only knew that, somehow, she managed to get both hands on the rope and it was towing her to safety.

Her feet hadn't yet touched bottom when Luke splashed into the water, circling her waist with one arm and pulling her to safety. Jo sagged against him as they stumbled along the rocky path toward the grass, where they both slid to the ground.

Two kayakers came downstream, eyeing them curiously. "Everything okay?" one of them asked.

Luke nodded. "We're fine, thanks." He pulled Jo close. "We're fine now," he said, one hand stroking her wet hair. "I thought I'd lost you."

Jo wrapped her arms around his neck, burrowing into his shoulder. "I thought I was going to drown."

His arm tightened around her. "You almost did. I've never been so scared in my life. I heard you scream and saw the bridge splintered. Why in the world did you try to cross it?"

"I saw you on the other side. I thought you'd used it so it was safe."

"I ride over there, so I take the new one. The only time I've crossed that old bridge recently was the last time I had to chase you through the trees."

Jo raised her head to look at him. "I guess you must think I'm really stupid."

"Stupid? No." Luke slipped his hand along her cheek to cup her chin. "Maybe just curious." His gaze moved to her lips. "Are you?"

Jo felt herself begin to tremble and she didn't think it had anything to do with her near-death experience.

Strange sensations were racing along her arms and legs like static electricity, sending tingles everywhere. And she knew, with some newfound intuition, that Luke was going to kiss her.

She hoped her voice didn't sound as shaky as she felt. "Yes."

Luke inched forward and slowly covered her mouth with his.

Time stopped for Jo as Luke's kiss lingered. The world went totally silent. Only the two of them existed. This kiss was nothing like the light brushing he had given her two years ago. His lips were soft but firm, the pressure gentle but insistent, making her insides go all mushy. Jo breathed into the kiss, her mouth yielding to his. The surprise of his tongue touching the tip of hers startled Jo, but the sensation quickly turned into something completely pleasant…and he tasted so good.

Luke deepened the kiss, swirling his tongue around hers. He pulled back and finished with a light sweep across her lips. "I…probably shouldn't have done that."

"No," Jo stammered. "I mean, yes." Why did her lips feel so swollen that she could hardly talk? "I mean…I wanted you to."

A corner of his mouth lifted up. "Because you were curious?"

"No. Well, yes. I mean…" She let her voice trail off.

Luke tilted his head. "What do you mean?"

Jo felt her face grow warm, but she might as well be truthful. "I…like it. I want to do it again."

Luke's eyes gazed into hers, their amber color turning dark and then he sighed. "I think I'd better get you home."

****

A week later Jo still tingled in strange places when she thought of Luke's kiss. Embarrassment and guilt followed the memory, but she couldn't stop thinking about it.

Lying in the hammock—Aunt Viv insisted she rest every afternoon to recover—Jo thought about how she'd made a fine mess of things. When Luke had brought her home, still soaked, Aunt Viv had nearly fainted. After her aunt's initial fright at Jo's near-drowning, she'd asked if Jo had been depressed. It had taken both her and Luke—Luke mostly—to convince her aunt that Jo had had no intentions of jumping off the bridge. She felt guilty about worrying her aunt.

But Jo felt guiltier about kissing Luke. He had a girlfriend.

Luke had stayed away this past week. Did he feel guilty too? Embarrassment washed over Jo as she thought about telling him she wanted him to kiss her again. Maybe he thought she was one of those fast, easy girls like Ruby. Or even Mary Anne. After all, Mary Anne had told Jo to go ahead and meet Luke at the cabin. Jo had an inkling now of what could happen there. Not that she would consider doing…whatever it was. No. But she was curious. Luke had definitely been right about that.

Heat seared across Jo's face as embarrassment doused her once more. Luke hadn't kissed her again, so he probably regretted what happened, since he had a girlfriend.

Jo sighed, feeling restless. Her aunt thought these afternoons in the hammock were relaxing, but Jo would have felt better doing something. Wendy had ridden over to see the twins. Mary Anne had driven into town to pick up brown sugar from the grocery store for a batch of cookies Aunt Viv wanted to make. Maybe Jo should have gone into town with her cousin...not that Mary Anne had invited her.

A few minutes later, Jo heard the crunch of gravel as Mary Anne returned from town. Jo got up and walked toward the house. Helping her aunt with the cookies would give her something to do.

"Did you get the brown sugar?" she asked Mary Anne.

"Yeah. Here." Mary Anne held out a paper bag. "Oh, wait." She opened the bag and took out a folded piece of paper. "This is mine." She stuck it in her pocket and then held the bag out again and smiled at Jo. "I brought some candy too. Take your pick. I'm going to put the car in the garage."

"Thanks." Watching her cousin walk away, Jo wondered why she was being so friendly.

****

"What's with her?' Wendy asked Jo two days later when Mary Anne had actually let them borrow *December's Children*, one of her favorite Stones albums, before leaving for town. "Usually, she'd just tell us to get off her cloud."

"I don't know," Jo replied, putting the LP on the hi-fi. "She's really been in a good mood lately."

"Yeah. That's not like her." Wendy looked thoughtful. "She even promised to bring back my favorite candy from the store. I sure hope she remembers."

"Which won't be soon," Jo said. "I heard Mary Anne ask if she could meet Ruby for a pizza before coming home."

"Geez. Do you think she'll bring some home for us?"

"Probably not. Besides, who wants cold pizza?"

"Yeah, I guess you're right. Maybe Mom will let us get some tomorrow."

"Get some what?" Aunt Viv asked as she came into the living room and sat down.

"Pizza," Wendy answered. "You let Mary Anne get some."

"We'll see," her mother said. "Could you turn off the hi-fi? It's time for the news. I want to find out if the riots in Los Angeles have stopped yet."

Obligingly, Wendy picked the needle up and placed the arm on its holder. "I don't understand why people are burning and looting everything there."

Aunt Viv sighed. "Sometimes people let their emotions get the best of them and they don't think straight."

"A man was arrested for drunk driving. He wasn't supposed to be driving."

"It's more complicated than that, dear. Black people have not always been treated fairly."

"But President Johnson signed the Civil Rights Act last year. We learned that in history class," Jo said.

"That's true, but it takes a long time to change some people's minds about things," Aunt Viv answered and then shook her head as pictures of burning buildings came on the screen. "Such a waste."

"Maybe Dr. King will go there and fix it," Wendy said.

"Let's hope so," her mother replied, "but right now, I want each of you to listen carefully. You're witnessing history in the making."

Jo would have preferred not to watch the violence, but she remembered her mother saying archeologists had to painstakingly examine each relic they found and couldn't jump to conclusions—and neither should people. She settled back on the sofa as different commentators—black and white—talked about what was happening and why. Finally, the ten o'clock news finished with announcing that Dr. King would indeed be coming to Los Angeles.

Aunt Viv switched the TV off and then frowned as she glanced at the clock on the wall. "Mary Anne should have been back by now."

"Maybe she and Ruby got to talking and forgot what time it is," Jo said.

"Mary Anne left at four o'clock. I told her to be back before dark."

Jo exchanged an uneasy glance with Wendy. It had been dark for two hours.

"Maybe Mary Anne and Ruby are driving around in Ken's souped-up car and forgot the time," Wendy said. "You know how they like to circle around and around the town square looking cool."

That suggestion made her aunt's frown increase. "I specifically told her not to hang around with those boys."

"Mary Anne doesn't always listen to what you say, Mom."

"I know." Her mother sighed. "I'm going to have to have another talk with her." She looked from Wendy to Jo. "Did she say anything to either of you about plans other than meeting Ruby for pizza?"

Jo shook her head, although a thought niggled at her. Mary Anne had slipped a note into her pocket the other day when she'd come home from town. Had she made arrangements to meet Bob? Maybe that was why she'd been in such a good mood. But then, Mary Anne would have deliberately lied to her mother.

"Nope," Wendy said. "The last thing Mary Anne said was that she'd bring us my favorite chocolate candy on her way home."

A look of concern crossed her mother's face as she got up. "I'm going to call the constable and ask him to be on the lookout for my car."

Wendy waited until her mother had gone into the kitchen where the phone was. Then she turned to Jo. "Mary Anne is going to be *so* grounded. I'll bet Mom doesn't let her go anywhere until school starts!"

"I hope—"

A heavy crash interrupted Jo. She and Wendy jumped from their chairs and ran to the kitchen. Aunt Viv was leaning against the counter while the phone's receiver dangled against the wall. Two plates lay shattered on the floor where her aunt must have knocked them from the countertop.

"What's wrong, Mom?" Wendy asked as she hurried over, Jo directly behind her.

"My car." Her mother's voice broke and she cleared her throat. "The constable said my car's been parked by the bakery since this afternoon."

"That's good," Jo said, feeling relieved. "They just forgot the time."

Aunt Viv shook her head. "The bakery closed early today because the oven broke down."

"Then where is Mary Anne?" Wendy asked.

Her mother gripped the counter, her knuckles turning white. "Your sister seems to be missing."

Chapter Twenty

People packed the parlor the next afternoon. Jo wedged herself through the crowd to sit on the sofa beside her aunt and Wendy. Aunt Viv had called the twins' father last night and Tommy had contacted the riding club. They'd just returned from searching the area. The county sheriff and the town constable were at the house as well, asking questions and taking notes. So far, nothing had turned up.

Aunt Viv, bleary-eyed from lack of sleep, looked dazed. Amy brought her a cup of black coffee.

"My mom always says coffee helps."

"Thanks, dear." Aunt Viv took a sip, but the cup rattled in her hand so much she put it down. "I'll try to finish it later."

The sheriff walked over. "Your daughter told you she was meeting a friend for pizza. Did she say anything else? About where else she might go?"

"No. Nothing."

"Did she get a phone call before she left? Maybe from another friend?"

Aunt Viv shook her head. "We've only got the wall phone in the kitchen. I was in there most of the afternoon."

"Is your daughter dating anyone?"

"No." Aunt Viv hesitated. "At least, she shouldn't be."

The sheriff looked at Jo and Wendy. "Did Mary Anne say anything to either of you about a boyfriend?"

"She used to date Tim." Wendy gave him a dark look. "But they broke off—"

"A long time ago," Carla interrupted.

"Just a few months ago," Wendy countered, glowering at both of them.

"Did your sister take it hard?" the sheriff asked. "At least hard enough to run away, maybe?"

Aunt Viv gasped. "You think she ran away? Why?"

The constable came over. "Just a possibility, ma'am. We haven't found any trace of her. We've searched everywhere, even the woods."

"How about the cabin?" Jo asked.

Amy looked confused. "What cabin?"

"It's a stone hut not far from the river," Luke replied and then nodded to Jo. "I remember you saying it'd been used, so it was the first place I looked."

"I should have known you'd check it out," Jo said.

"Anything I can do," Luke answered, his face intent. "Just let me know."

Amy frowned slightly, then turned to the constable. "Mary Anne had the car. If she were going to run away, why wouldn't she drive?"

"Too easy to get caught. We'd put an APB out immediately." He looked at his notepad. "The twins gave me a list. These boys—Ken Wheeler, Frank Canton, Bob Colby—any of them that she might have run off with?"

Jo looked at her aunt and then at the constable. "Bob maybe. I saw...I saw Mary Anne sneak in late a couple of times. I thought it was his car at the end of the road."

Aunt Viv moaned softly. "I thought I'd convinced her not to see him."

"It's a lead, ma'am. Do any of you have an idea where they might go?"

"Mary Anne said she wanted to move to Minneapolis," Wendy offered and took her mother's hand when she started to cry.

"That's such a big place," Aunt Viv whispered. "Anything could happen—"

"Mrs. Wade." Luke stepped forward. "I know you don't like Bob, but the guy has street smarts. If…*if* Mary Anne ran off with him, he'll be sure she stays safe."

"You…you think so?"

"Yes." Luke glanced at Jo briefly and turned his attention back to her aunt. "When a guy really likes a girl, he'll want to take care of her. I think Bob's got it in him to do that."

The constable snapped his notepad shut and headed for the door. "I'll go check out his place. If he's gone, I'll make some calls."

Aunt Viv wiped at her tears. "Thank you."

"You betcha."

"One more thing." The sheriff walked toward the door too. "Even though we didn't see any signs of foul play, it's possible your daughter may have been abducted. Call us immediately if a ransom note arrives. The sooner we can act on it, the better our chances are."

"Abducted?" Aunt Viv repeated, staring at the closed door. "Who would want to kidnap Mary Anne?"

No one had an answer, and from the stricken looks on most of the riding group's faces as they filed out, Jo was pretty sure they didn't want to talk about it either.

Only Luke stayed, although Jo saw Amy waiting for him on the porch.

"I'm going to keep looking. We'll find Mary Anne,"

Luke said. "There's something that must have been missed in the search."

But what? Jo thought as Luke left. What?

****

The next morning Aunt Viv and Wendy went into town to talk with the constable again. Neither Bob nor his uncle had been home yesterday, but a note had been tacked on their door saying they'd gone fishing. That sounded "fishy" to Jo, but the constable said it wasn't that unusual. Lots of folks went Up North to one of the bigger lakes this time of year. Still, he'd put out an APB for the uncle's truck and asked Aunt Viv to come in to complete paperwork that would officially declare Mary Anne a missing person. Jo had wanted to go with them, but her aunt had asked her to stay home, just in case… She didn't say for what.

Jo went upstairs to get her transistor and paused by Mary Anne's door. She opened it slowly, half-hoping, half-praying that Mary Anne had snuck home last night and would be in bed with the covers pulled over her head.

The room was empty, the bed halfway made, which was how Mary Anne usually left it. The room was a mess. A couple of pairs of shoes lay on the floor and a bunch of clothes had been heaped on the chair by the closet. Jo remembered the note Mary Anne had put in the pocket of her jeans a few days ago and went to the chair. Rummaging through the pile of clothes, Jo finally found the pair her cousin had been wearing. She stuck her hand inside, breathing a sigh of relief when her fingers found the paper. She pulled the note out and unfolded it.

Hey, baby,

I'll pick you up in town Tuesday and we'll go to that place in the woods.

Bob

Jo stared at the note. Today was Wednesday, which meant Mary Anne had gone to town yesterday to meet Bob, not Ruby. But it didn't explain why she was missing. Besides, Luke said he'd searched the cabin.

Jo heard the cantering of a horse on the yard road and went to the window. To her surprise, Amy was coming up the road. Alone. What in the world for? Sticking the note into her pocket, Jo hurried down the stairs and out the front door.

"Did you hear anything?" she asked as Amy dismounted and walked toward her. For once she wasn't smiling.

"I guess it depends on what you mean."

"About Mary Anne." *Who else would they be looking for?* "Did you hear anything?"

"Not about Mary Anne." Amy mounted the steps to stand beside Jo. "But I did hear something regarding Luke."

Luke. Jo's stomach felt like Flame had really kicked her. Had someone told Amy that Jo had a crush on him? No one knew they'd kissed. No one had seen them…the hair at Jo's nape prickled. The kayakers. Had they continued on down the river or had they pulled in on the opposite shore? Jo couldn't remember. But what if someone had seen her kissing Luke and told Amy?

"I want to talk to you," Amy said.

Jo swallowed hard. "About what?"

Amy gave her a steady look. "About Luke."

Jo felt suddenly uneasy. The countryside was quiet. Not even a car crunched the gravel on the road. They were alone out here.

"Can we go inside?" Amy asked.

"I…ah…actually, I was headed to the barn. Ah… What about Luke?"

Amy tilted her head to one side and studied her. "I think you know." She sighed. "Luke told me about the kiss."

Luke had told Amy about the kiss? Why? And how angry was Amy? Jo had never seen her so serious or solemn before. "I can explain—"

"I don't think kisses can be explained," Amy said.

"I was scared. I'd almost drowned. It…it just happened. It…it won't happen again."

"I think it will."

"No. I haven't even seen Luke since then. Well, except for yesterday, and you were here."

"Yes. I heard what he said about a guy wanting to take care of a girl he cares about."

"But he meant you!"

Amy shook her head. "Luke's never said that to me. And he didn't tell me about the cabin, either."

"Wendy's the one who showed me the cabin. Even Mary Anne knows about it."

"It doesn't matter."

"But…"

Amy held up her hand to silence Jo. "I came over here to tell you two things. The first is that Luke told me he likes you too much for us to continue dating. The second is that I was going to break up with Luke anyway. I saw the way he looked at you yesterday. There have been other times, too." She took a deep breath. "My mom's always told me it takes two people to make a relationship work and not to settle for anyone who doesn't think I'm the most important person in his life. I'm not that person for Luke."

Jo stared at her. "And you think I am?"

Amy shrugged and walked down the steps toward her horse. "I don't know," she said as she mounted. "I'm just not willing to settle for anything less than someone who wants only me. See you around."

As Amy rode off without looking back, Jo sagged against the porch rail, speechless. In the last twenty-four hours, her world had turned topsy-turvy. She felt giddy and guilty. Guilty because she felt giddy. Mary Anne was missing and that's all Jo should be concentrating on. But giddiness overtook her. Luke and Amy weren't dating anymore. Maybe Jo should feel guilty about that too, but she couldn't. Luke had told Amy about the kiss! He'd told her that he liked Jo! What would she do when she saw him again?

Excitement rippled through her and she did a little dance, only to stop at the sight of the mailman turning his car on to the yard road. He never delivered the mail to the door, since their box was at the road.

He got out of his car, although he left the engine running. "Thought I'd better bring this right up, since it's marked 'Urgent.' Is Mrs. Wade here?"

"She's in town." Jo held her hand out for the letter. "I'll see that she gets this as soon as she gets back."

"All right then. Gotta be going."

Jo looked at the envelope after he left. It was addressed to her aunt in uneven penmanship, as though someone were writing with the wrong hand. It had no return address. *Urgent*. Should she open it? She hesitated, feeling guilty about opening her aunt's mail. Mary Anne supposedly ran off with Bob, but what if she didn't? What if this was a ransom note? The sheriff had said that could be a possibility. Jo's hand began to tremble as she ripped the envelope open, then sagged against the porch rail once more. Not only had Mary Anne been abducted, but the kidnapper wanted his money this afternoon or he'd take her out of the state.

Jo's watch said it was nearly noon. Who knew how long it would take Aunt Viv at the constable's office. Her aunt needed this information now. Besides, the bank was in town. There was only one thing Jo could do. She straightened, took a deep breath, and headed for the barn.

She would have to ride into town.

****

Jo pushed her trepidations aside as she saddled Flame. This was no time to give in to her fear about riding again. She just had to do it. Still, she was aware of how her pulse raced and her breathing shallowed. Strangely enough, once Flame got to the end of the yard road, Jo's anxiety lessened. Flame had always had a gentle disposition, and the mare walked calmly now. Jo began to relax. Nothing bad was going to happen at this pace. She didn't want to push Flame into a trot or canter, even though the vet had said her legs were healed. Better to plod along.

Jo reined Flame over to the side of the road at the sound of a truck approaching from behind. When it slowed, she turned to look and saw Luke at the wheel. Thoughts of her earlier conversation with Amy rushed through Jo's mind, but this was no time to bring that up.

"Where are you going?" Luke asked as he idled the truck.

"I—my aunt—just got a ransom note." Jo waved the letter. "Aunt Viv's at the constable's office and I've got to get this to her right away. The kidnapper wants money by this afternoon."

"Here, let me have it," Luke said as he held out his hand. "I can drive there a lot faster than you can get there on Flame."

"True." Jo handed him the letter. "Thanks."

"Sure. I'll come over later, if that's all right? I'd like to talk to you."

Tingles slivered down Jo's spine in anticipation. Her excitement must have affected her hands because Flame tossed her head. "I'd like that," Jo said as she stroked the mare's neck to calm the horse—and herself.

"See you later then." Luke shifted gears and drove off.

Jo watched until the truck disappeared around a curve and turned Flame back. They had nearly reached the yard road when Jo decided to ride longer. Maybe then, by the time she returned home, she'd have gotten over her fear of being on a horse again. Even now, the feeling was rapidly fading.

They continued on for another mile, finally coming to the new bridge that crossed the river. A narrow path beside the bridge led down to the water. Since she was testing herself, she might as well get closer to the water too. She hadn't been to the river since the near drowning.

Jo dismounted and led Flame down for a drink, then dropped the reins so the mare could graze. She settled herself on a flat boulder well away from the muddy bank. The granite, warmed by the sun, felt good. The river at this point flowed much less swiftly, perhaps because it had just come around a bend and widened as well. The scene felt tranquil and Jo let herself think.

Something about the two notes didn't add up. Jo could understand Bob sending Mary Anne a note to meet him in town and they'd go to the cabin. Mary Anne had all but admitted that they'd gone there before. But why put a Gone Fishing sign on the farmhouse door? Unless…maybe they'd made plans to run away together. Jo tried to remember if Mary Anne's cosmetics had been on the dresser or if any clothing was missing when she'd gone to her room earlier. It would be hard to tell, as messy as the room had been.

Since Bob had a car, it would make sense for Mary Anne to leave her mother's car parked where it could be found. The keys had been under the floor mat. Jo couldn't imagine doing something like that in Brooklyn, but it hadn't seemed to raise any red flags here in farming country.

But then why the ransom note? The kidnapper wanted two thousand dollars in small bills and would call that afternoon about where to leave it. Two thousand dollars was enough to live on at least six months, maybe more. Jo knew her aunt had that much because she'd just collected the rents from her acreage in July. But how would the kidnapper know that? Most folks would need some time to get that amount of money. Unless… Jo sat up abruptly, nearly slipping off the smooth stone.

Unless Bob was the kidnapper. If Mary Anne intended to run away with him, maybe she'd told him about the rent. Neither one of them had a job, so they'd need money to live on, at least until they could find work. That made sense.

But where would they be hiding? The constable said the farmhouse was empty. The note said they'd go to the cabin, but Luke had searched the cabin. Jo frowned, remembering the note hadn't said "cabin" It had said "into the woods." The sheriff said they'd searched the woods, though, so where else…

The cave.

Jo knew Mary Anne followed her and Wendy sometimes when they went to the cabin, but she didn't know if Mary Anne had followed them when they'd explored the cave. Still, someone had been using the cabin nearby. There were drinking parties down by the old bridge—Jo felt pretty sure Bob drank and smoked cigarettes—so it was possible he'd found the cave. Tucked away, it made the perfect hiding place.

Jo jumped to her feet and led Flame back up the path, then rode across the bridge. She knew where to pick up the trail that followed the riverbank, since it was the one Luke had taken bringing her back after the accident.

Within minutes, she arrived at the base of the Indian mound where the massive boulders were clustered. Dropping Flame's reins once more, Jo climbed the rocks, maneuvering along the ledge until she could see the entrance to the cave. A faint scent of Mary Anne's perfume wafted out.

"I knew you'd be here!" Jo said as she entered. She heard shuffling and moved forward carefully, her eyes not yet adjusted to the darkness. "You've got to come out. Aunt Viv is worried sick—"

"That's too bad," a harsh voice said as rough hands grabbed her and pushed her to the ground, "but it looks as though I'll have to increase the ransom."

Chapter Twenty-One

As Jo fell, she rolled onto her back to kick at her assailant. He only laughed and grabbed an ankle, giving it a vicious twist. Jo cried out in pain and tried to crawl away, but the man caught her. He flipped her onto her stomach and tied her hands behind her with his belt, then gave her a none-too-gentle shove toward Mary Anne, who sat huddled against the stone wall, gagged and with her hands and feet bound.

Jo's ankle throbbed and she could already feel it swelling, but at least her eyes had gotten accustomed to the light. She got her first good look at the kidnapper. Not Bob. This man was older, with shaggy gray hair and a beard. "Who are you?" she asked as she pushed herself up beside Mary Anne and tried to adjust to the rocky edges sticking out. "Why are you doing this?"

He leaned against the rocks by the entrance. "You ask a lot of questions that ain't your business."

Jo tried to think of what Emma Peel would do. She often posed as a reporter, but on the TV show she always got answers to her questions. "Why did you abduct Mary Anne? Was she at the wrong place at the wrong time?"

"Like I said, too many questions." The man pulled out a dirty handkerchief and held it up. "Shut up or I'll gag you like I did your friend there. She talked too much too."

Mary Anne made a muffled sound, her eyes huge as

an owl's. Jo clamped her mouth shut. Emma Peel's other talents were fencing and martial arts. Jo didn't have a sword and she didn't know karate, either. So much for trying to act like a television heroine. Things like that didn't work in real life, but Jo could stay calm and keep her wits about her. Emma sure would do that…and she'd look for a weapon she could use.

First she had to get her hands loose. The leather on the belt was stiff and, in his haste, the man had done a quick loop around Jo's wrists and a fold-over, pulling the strap through the loop. Just like cinching a saddle. If she hadn't been in so much pain from her ankle, she might have smiled. She could undo this.

But she needed to divert the man's attention from her movements. She needed to get him to talk. Asking questions hadn't worked, but maybe…if she *acted* sympathetic…

"Something really bad must have happened to you."

"Ain't nothin' bad…" The man narrowed his eyes at her. "Why do you say that?"

Jo stilled her hands. She'd gotten the belt to loosen a little. "You look unhappy."

"I'll be real happy when I get the ransom."

"Do you need money?"

The man laughed. "Who don't?"

If she could get him to talking…she needed just a little more wiggle room. "You're right. We all do, but…"

"But what?"

"Isn't this…this kidnapping…a pretty dangerous way to do it?"

"I've done dangerous things before."

"But have you ever kidnapped someone?" There! She'd gotten her hand loose.

He paused. "No. I ain't never done that."

"I didn't think so. You don't look mean."

"I ain't."

"Well…" Jo closed her hand over a loose rock behind her. "Would you be nice enough to take that gag out of Mary Anne's mouth? She looks really uncomfortable."

"She'll start screaming again."

Jo looked at Mary Anne, who shook her head frantically. "I don't think she will."

The man hesitated, then shook his head. "Nope. I ain't takin' no chances. Fact is, I'm getting me to the gas station down the road where I can make another phone call. Neither of you is going anywhere, and time's a-wastin'." He looked around the small cave. "Ain't nothing here to help you escape, either. I'll be back."

Even though she could hear the man's footsteps fading, Jo forced herself to count to ten slowly and then count again before she moved. She pulled the gag down from Mary Anne's face and turned her cousin so she could untie her hands.

"How did you get loose?" Mary Anne asked.

"Never mind. Do you know who that man is?"

"He's Bob's uncle. Not the one who's living here. One that came from Chicago a couple of weeks ago. Bob said—"

"Never mind. We don't have time to talk right now. You've got to go and get help."

Mary Anne furrowed her brows as Jo undid the rope around her cousin's legs. "We'll both go."

Jo shook her head. "I can't. I don't know if my foot is broken or not, but I know I can't put any weight on it. I sure can't climb down rocks or mount Flame. You've got to go."

"But I can't just leave you here."

"You have to. Flame's grazing by the riverbank. Turn her around and keep the reins loose. She'll head home."

"But—"

"Hurry. We don't know if he'll change his mind and come back."

"But what if I meet him on the road?"

"We'll just have to take that chance. Now *go*."

Mary Anne gave her a troubled glance. "I think—"

"*Go!*"

Her cousin bit her lip and then she nodded. "I'll get help."

Jo managed to hold herself steady while she listened to her cousin scrambling down the rocks. When all finally fell silent, her body began to tremble. Mary Anne was no horsewoman. Even if she were, Flame could only walk. It was almost a mile to the bridge and then four miles into town on a road the kidnapper might very well be on as well. Would Mary Anne make it? Even if she did, would the police get here before the kidnapper came back?

Jo picked up the loose rock she'd intended to use on the man and crawled to the cave's entrance. She couldn't maneuver onto the ledge because it required standing, but maybe she could hide in a crevice outside, on the other side of the cave.

Painfully, she hauled herself over the jutting rocks, trying not to hit her injured ankle on too many jagged edges. She shook with the effort by the time she managed to wedge between two smaller boulders. She was hidden from the view of anyone at the cave's entrance, but she could still be seen from the ground if the kidnapper looked up.

Jo held the rock she'd taken from the cave in her hands and prayed the man wouldn't look up when he returned.

****

The throbbing of her ankle made Jo lose track of time, but she didn't think it had been that long when she heard tire wheels crunching on the gravel road not far from the riverbank. Could the police be arriving already? Jo held her breath as she heard footsteps below and then tried to wedge farther between the rocks when she spotted the shaggy gray head of the kidnapper.

Had he met Mary Anne on the road? She wasn't with him, but maybe she had been tied up in his car or, worse, knocked unconscious and put in the trunk. Jo could hear the man climbing up the rocks on the other side. In a minute, he'd be at the cave entrance. She sucked in her breath again and waited.

The man bellowed with rage. Loose rock bounced off the boulders as he came back outside. "Show yourself," he shouted. "Don't make me come find you. You'll be sorry if you do."

Jo shrank back, scarcely daring to breathe.

"You can't have gone far," the man muttered. He wasn't shouting, but he sounded closer. *Dear Lord, help me*. The man was coming toward her. She could hear more stones rattling. In another minute, he'd spot the small overhang where she sat. Jo clenched her rock. If he came at her, she'd smash his face.

"There you are, you stupid girl." The man loomed large, only a few feet from her. "Maybe I'll just break your other ankle to teach you a lesson! Now come here—

" *Whoosh*! His breath left him as he suddenly toppled sideways, lost his footing, and tumbled down the rocks. His body landed with a heavy thud on the ground, and he lay still.

Luke appeared where the man had just been and edged around the rock to kneel by Jo. "Did he hurt you?"

Jo stared at Luke, not quite sure if he was real.

He touched her shoulder. "Jo? Are you all right?"

The touch brought her out of her haze. "My ankle. I don't know if it's broken. He twisted it pretty bad."

Luke muttered something she couldn't hear and put his hands on her calf, running his fingers very lightly along the sides, taking extra care around her foot. "I think it's just a bad sprain, but the doc needs to look at it."

"How did you—"

"Dang it!" Luke said as the man below started to groan. "I hoped he'd stay out until the cops get here."

Jo put a hand on his arm. "There's rope in the cave. And a belt. He tied us."

Luke's jaw hardened and his eyes darkened as he rose. "I'll be right back."

In short order, Luke had the man hog-tied and gagged with the man's own dirty handkerchief. He did it with such expertise, Jo wondered if he'd ever been in a rodeo. But the thought left her as Luke scrambled up the rocks and then picked her up with ease. She wrapped her arms around his neck as he carefully started sidestepping back down.

"Don't fall," Jo said, then realized that sounded pretty stupid. She felt the rumbling in Luke's chest and knew he was laughing.

"I'll try not to. Just hang on."

As if she needed to be told. She'd never felt so safe

in her life, even though the kidnapper was glaring at both of them from his trussed position. Luke walked a good distance away from the man before he knelt and placed Jo on the ground. Taking off his jacket, he bunched it up and placed it beneath her ankle. Then he put an arm around her shoulder and pulled her close.

Jo nestled against him. "How did you find me?"

"Tracks."

"Tracks?"

Luke grinned. "Remember I told you Dad made me go to Indian camp?"

"Yes, but—"

"I rode over to your place after I delivered the ransom note. When I didn't see Flame in the barn, I figured you'd decided to continue riding, so I went back to the road. Flame had special shoes put on her forefeet, so it wasn't hard to pick out their tracks."

"But how did you know where I was going?"

"I didn't. I got as far as the bridge and saw you'd gone down to the bank. That scared me a little. Then I saw Mary Anne coming over the bridge riding your horse." Luke kissed the top of Jo's head. "That really scared me."

Jo nestled closer, her arm around Luke's waist. "So Mary Anne made it. I was afraid the kidnapper would find her."

"She probably just missed him. She told me where you were, and I saw a car cross over the bridge a couple of minutes later." Luke pointed to the man. "I didn't know it was that jerk until I saw the same car when I got here."

"I'm lucky you were right behind him."

"I'm glad I got here in time." Luke stroked Jo's hair.

"I don't know…" The wail of sirens drowned out his voice as the sheriff and constable both pulled up, lights flashing on their cars, with the ambulance right behind them.

"We'll have to talk later," Luke said.

Jo smiled. "I'm looking forward to it."

****

Later that evening, Jo sat on the sofa in the parlor, her ankle taped—it was a bad sprain after all—and elevated on the coffee table with a pillow. Luke sat beside her, holding her hand. Mary Anne huddled in a big armchair next to the sofa, her face pale, but Wendy practically bounced in the chair across from them.

"Tell me everything that happened!"

"Perhaps this isn't the best time." Aunt Viv still held the tissue box she'd been using to wipe her tears since they'd all gotten back from the hospital. "Even the police said an official report could wait until morning."

"No." Mary Anne straightened up in her chair. "I want to talk."

"Are you sure?"

She nodded. "Since you grounded me, I hadn't been able to see Bob, but I sent him a letter a couple of weeks ago. I guess it was about the time George, his other uncle, arrived. Anyway, the day I went into town, the guy at the pizza place said a note had been left for me. It was from Bob—at least, I thought it was—asking me to meet him in town. We were going to go out to the cabin later."

"So you were the one using the cabin?" Wendy asked.

"Sometimes." Mary Anne glanced at her mother. "I knew you didn't want me to see him, but he's really nice—"

"This isn't the time to discuss that," Aunt Viv said, "but I don't understand why Bob would want to kidnap you."

Mary Anne shook her head. "He didn't even know what was going on. Bob and his other uncle, Bill, had gone to Minneapolis for special car parts and were going to stay for some auto show."

"So Bob didn't write the note?" Jo asked.

"No. His uncle George did."

Aunt Viv frowned. "But why?"

"I guess for the money," Mary Anne replied. "He told me his brother Bill had mentioned harvest time was when the farmers paid their rents for our acreage and maybe Bob could persuade me to take them all out on the town one night."

"So if Bob didn't meet you yesterday, what happened?" Wendy asked.

"George was there. He said something about Bob trying to get his car to work and asked him to come into town to pick me up. It made sense since we were going to drive to the cabin, so I believed him." Mary Anne bit her lip. "I was so stupid."

"Not stupid," Jo said, remembered the note she'd gotten two years ago that she thought was from Luke. She'd done the same thing. "Sometimes we're just gullible."

Mary Anne gave her a watery smile. "I'm sorry I've been so mean to you. I was the one who sent you that nasty letter, and yet you saved my life."

Jo's face heated. "You kinda saved mine, too, by telling Luke where I was."

"Still, you were brave."

"Not really. I thought you were with Bob and that

the two of you were going to run away. I just wanted to stop you."

Mary Anne's eyes widened. "I'd never run away with anybody."

"Will you give me your promise on that?" Aunt Viv asked. "I feel like I'm about to have a nervous breakdown."

"I promise. But, Mom, I really wish you'd let me date Bob. He's not like you think he is."

"She's right, Mrs. Wade," Luke interjected. "Bob's had some rough patches, but one of the reasons he moved from Chicago was to get away from people like his uncle George. Bob's a pretty decent guy, deep down."

Aunt Viv swallowed hard. "Perhaps I've been a bit too harsh."

"Thanks, Mom! Bob will be so surprised when he gets back."

"I'll consider it," her mother said, "but I want to meet his uncle—Bill, not George—before I agree."

Mary Anne gave her mother a big smile. "Yes, ma'am!"

"And now, I think we all need to get to bed," Aunt Viv said firmly. "We do have to go into town tomorrow to take care of the paperwork."

Mary Anne rose and yawned. "No argument from me."

"I think I'll talk to Jo a while," Wendy said.

"Tomorrow will be time enough for you to talk to her," her mother answered, glancing over at Luke. "I suspect someone else needs to talk to her tonight."

****

As soon as everyone had cleared the parlor, Luke put his arm around Jo's shoulders. "I thought they'd never leave."

She leaned against him. "Me either."

"We need to talk, Jo."

"About Amy?"

"Yes. We had a talk yesterday. Things hadn't been going so well between us this summer and, bottom line, she broke up with me."

"Hmmm. I know."

"You know?"

Jo sat up and turned toward Luke. "Amy came by yesterday morning and told me—only she said you were the one who broke it off."

"It's really not important who did."

"Amy said she didn't feel she was the most important person in your life."

"She's right. She's not."

"Of course, she didn't mean your dad or family..."

"I know what she meant. We hit it off because we both had Arabians and then the Sadie Hawkins dance came up and we just sort of started dating. I enjoyed her company—"

"You don't have to tell me this, Luke. I think Amy is a really nice person."

He nodded. "She is. A lot of girls would have been really mad if they were told there was someone else."

Jo's breath hitched. She knew what Amy had said, but she needed to hear it from Luke. "Someone else?"

"You." He raised his hand to trace the curve of her cheek with his fingers. "I liked you when I first met you two years ago, but you were so young."

"I was really silly, too."

"But in a nice way. Anyway, when you came back in June, I thought we could be friends, but each time I saw you, I wanted to spend more time with you. And then, when you almost drowned, I knew a part of me would have died that day too."

"And the kiss?"

Luke smiled. "I think the kiss would have happened eventually. Almost losing you just made it happen faster."

"I don't want to lose you either, Luke."

"For sure?"

"For sure."

Luke drew her closer. "Then maybe we should seal that promise with a kiss."

Jo put her arms around his neck. "I think so too."

And this kiss was full of promise.

A word about the author...

Cynthia Breeding lives on the Gulf Coast of Texas with a very non-spoiled poodle-mix and enjoys walking and horseback-riding on the beach, as well as sailing.

www.cynthiabreeding.com